VAMPIRE HUNTER D

Other *Vampire Hunter D* books published by
Dark Horse Books and Digital Manga Publishing

VAMPIRE HUNTER D

VOLUME 4
TALE OF THE DEAD TOWN

Written by
HIDEYUKI KIKUCHI

Illustrations by
YOSHITAKA AMANO

English translation by
KEVIN LEAHY

Dark Horse Books®
Milwaukie

Los Angeles

VAMPIRE HUNTER D 4: TALE OF THE DEAD TOWN

Cover art by Yoshitaka Amano
English translation by Kevin Leahy
Book Design by Heidi Whitcomb

Published by
Dark Horse Books
a division of Dark Horse Comics
10956 SE Main Street
Milwaukie OR 97222
DarkHorse.com

Digital Manga Publishing
1487 West 178th Street, Suite 300
Gardena CA 90248
DMPBooks.com

Library of Congress Cataloging-in-Publication Data

Kikuchi, Hideyuki, 1949-
  [D--Shigaitan. English]
  Tale of the dead town / written by Hideyuki Kikuchi ; illustrated by Yoshitaka Amano ; English translation by Kevin Leahy. -- 1st Dark Horse Books ed.
      p. cm. -- (Vampire hunter D ; v. 4)
  ISBN: 978-1-59582-093-8
  I. Amano, Yoshitaka. II. Leahy, Kevin. III. Title. IV. Series: Kikuchi, Hideyuki, 1949- Kyuketsuki hanta "D." ; v. 4.

  PL832.I37 K9813 2005 vol. 4
  895.6'36--dc22

                            2006016021

ISBN 978-1-59582-093-8

First printing: May 2006

10 9 8 7 6 5 4

Printed at Lake Book Manufacturing, Inc., Melrose Park, IL, USA

VAMPIRE HUNTER D

Journey by Night

CHAPTER I

I

On the Frontier, nothing was considered more dangerous than a journey by night.

Claiming the night was their world, the Nobility had once littered the globe with monsters and creatures of legend, as if to adorn the pitch-black with a touch of deadly beauty. Those same repugnant creatures ran rampant in the land of darkness to this very day. That was how the vampires bared their fangs at the human idea that held the light of day as the time for action and the dark of night for rest. The darkness of night was the greatest of truths, the vampires claimed, and the ruler of the world. *Farewell, white light of summer*.

That was why the night was filled with menace. The moans of dream demons lingered in the wind, and the darkness whispered the threats of dimension-ripping beasts. Just beyond the edge of the woods glowed eyes the color of jasper. So many eyes. Even well-armed troops sent into devastated sections of the Capital felt so relieved after they'd slipped through the blocks of dilapidated apartment complexes that they'd flop down right there on the road.

Out on the Frontier it was even worse. On the main roads, crude way stations had been built at intervals between one lodging place and the next. But, when the sun went down on one of the support roads linking the godforsaken villages, travelers were forced to defend themselves with nothing more than their own two hands and whatever weapons they could carry. There were only two beings that chose to travel by night. The Nobility. And dhampirs. Particularly if the dhampir was a Vampire Hunter.

Scattering a shower of moonlight far and wide, the shadowy form of a horse and rider climbed a desolate hill. The mount was just an average cyborg horse, but the features of the rider were as clean and clear as a jewel, like the strange beauty of the darkness and the moon crystallized. Every time the all-too-insistent wind touched him, it trembled with uncertainty, whirled, and headed off bearing a whole new air. Carrying a disquieting aura. His wide-brimmed traveler's hat, the ink-black cape and scarf darker than darkness, and the scabbard of the elegant longsword that adorned his back were all faded and worn enough to stir imaginings of the arduous times this traveler had seen.

The young traveler had his eyes closed, perhaps to avoid the wind-borne dust. His profile was so graceful it seemed the Master Craftsman in heaven above had made it His most exquisite work. The rider appeared to be thoroughly exhausted and immersed in a lonely sleep. Sleep—for him it was a mere break in the battle, but a far cry from peace of mind.

Something else mixed with the groaning of the wind. The traveler's eyes opened. A lurid light coursed into them, then quickly faded. His horse never broke its pace. A little over ten seconds was all they needed to reach the summit of the hill. Now the other sounds were clear. The crack of a gun and howls of wild beasts.

The traveler looked down at the plain below, spying a mid-sized motor home that was under attack. Several lesser dragons were prowling around it—more "children of the night" sown by the Nobility. Ordinarily, their kind dwelt in swamplands farther to the south, but occasionally problems with the weather controllers would send packs of dragons north. The migration of dangerous species was a serious problem on the Frontier.

The motor home was already half-wrecked. Holes had been ripped in the roofs of both the cab and the living quarters, and the lesser dragons kept sticking their heads in. The situation was clear just from the smoking scraps of wood, the sleeping bags, and a pair of partially eaten and barely recognizable human bodies lying in front of the motor home. Due to circumstances beyond their control—most likely something to do with their propulsion system—the family had been forced to camp out instead of sleeping in their vehicle like they should. But words couldn't begin to describe how foolhardy they'd been to expect one little campfire to keep the creatures that prowled the night at bay. There were three sleeping bags. But there weren't enough corpses to account for everyone.

Once again a gunshot rang out, a streak of orange from a window in the living quarters split the darkness, and one of the dragons reeled back as the spot between its eyes exploded. For someone foolish enough to camp out at night, the shooter seemed well informed and incredibly skilled with a gun. People who lived up north had usually never heard where to aim a kill shot on southern creatures like these lesser dragons. But a solution to that puzzle soon presented itself. There was a large magneto-bike parked beside the vehicle. Someone was pitching in to rescue them.

The rider tugged on the reins of his cyborg horse. Shaking off the moonlight that encrusted its body like so much dust, the horse suddenly began its descent. Galloping down the steep slope with the sort of speed normally reserved for level ground, the mount left a gale in its wake as it closed on the lesser dragons.

Noticing the headlong charge by this new foe, a dragon to the rear of the pack turned, and the horse and rider slipped by its side like a black wind. Bright blood didn't spout from between the creature's eyes until the horse had come to a sudden halt and the traveler had dismounted with a flourish of his cape. The way he walked toward the creatures—with their colossal maws gaping and rows of bloody teeth bared—seemed leisurely at first glance, but in due time showed the swiftness of a swallow in flight. All around the young man in black there was the sound of steel meeting steel time and time again. Unable to pull apart the jagged teeth they'd just brought together, each and every one of the lesser dragons around him collapsed in a bloody spray as gashes opened between their eyes. And the dragon leaping at him from the motor home's roof was no exception.

The young man's gorgeous countenance seemed weary of the cries of the dying creatures, but his expression didn't change in the slightest, and, without even glancing at the two mangled bodies, he returned his longsword to its sheath and headed back to his cyborg horse. As if to say he'd just done this on a lark, as if to suggest he didn't give a thought to the well-being of any survivors, he turned his back on this death-shrouded world and tightened his grip on the reins.

"Hey, wait a minute," a masculine voice called out in a somewhat agitated manner. The young man stopped and turned around. The vehicle's door opened and a bearded man in a leather vest appeared. In his right hand he held a single-shot armor-piercing rifle. A machete was tucked through his belt. With the grim countenance he sported, he'd have looked more natural holding the latter instead of a gun. "Not that I don't appreciate your help, bucko, but there's no account for you just turning and making tracks like that now. Come here for a minute."

"There's only one survivor," the young man said. "And it's a child, so you should be able to handle it alone."

A tinge of surprise flooded the other man's hirsute face. "How did you . . . ? Ah, you saw the sleeping bags. Now wait just a minute, bucko. The atomic reactor has a cracked heat exchanger and the whole motor home's lousy with radiation now. That's why the family went outside in the first place. The kid got a pretty good dose."

"Hurry up and take care of it then."

"The supplies I'm packing won't cut it. A town doctor's gotta see to this. Where are you headed, buddy? The Zemeckis rendezvous point?"

"That's right," the young man in black replied.

"Hold on. Just hold everything. I know the roads around here like the back of my hand."

"So do I." The young man turned away from the biker once again. Then he stopped. As he turned back, his eyes were eternally cold and dark.

The child was standing behind the biker. Her black hair would've hung past her waist if it hadn't been tied back by a rainbow-hued ribbon. The rough cotton shirt and long skirt did little to hide her age, or the swell of her full bosom. The girl was a beauty, around seventeen or eighteen years old. As she gazed at the young man, a curious hue of emotion filled her eyes. There was something in the gorgeous features of the youth that could make her forget the heart-rending loss of her family as well as the very real danger of losing her own life. Extending her hand, she was just about to say something when she crumpled to the ground face down.

"What did I tell you—she's hurt bad! She's not gonna last till dawn. That's why I need your help."

The youth wheeled his horse around without a word. "Which one of us will carry her?" he asked.

"Yours truly, of course. Getting you to help so far has been like pulling teeth, so I'll be damned if I'm gonna let you do the fun part."

The man got a leather belt off his bike and came back, then put the young woman on his back and cleverly secured her to himself. "Hands off," the man said, glaring at the youth in black as he straddled his magneto-bike. The girl fit perfectly into the seat behind him. It looked like quite a cozy arrangement. "Okay, here I go. Follow me." The man grabbed the handlebars, but before twisting the grip starter, he turned and said, "That's right— I didn't introduce myself, did I? I'm John M. Brasselli Pluto VIII."

"D."

"That's a good name you got there. Just don't go looking to shorten mine for something a little easier to say. When you call me, I'll thank you kindly to do it by my full name. John M. Brasselli Pluto VIII, okay?" But, while the man was driving his point home, D was looking to the skies. "What is it?" the biker asked.

"Things out there have caught the scent of blood and are on their way."

The black creatures framed against the moon were growing closer. A flock of avian predators. And lupine howls could be heard in the wind.

†

Expectations to the contrary, no threat materialized to hamper the party's progress. They rode for about three hours. When the hazy mountains far across the plain began to fill their field of view and take on a touch of reality, John M. Brasselli Pluto VIII turned his sharp gaze to D, who rode alongside him. "If we go to the foot of that there mountain, the town should be by. What business you got with them anyway, bucko?" he asked. When D made no answer he added, "Damn, playing the tough guy again I see. I bet you're used to just standing there doing the strong, silent type routine and getting all the ladies, chum. You're good at what you do, I'll give you that—just don't count on that always doing the trick for you. Sooner or later, it's always some straight-shooter like me that ends up the center of attention."

D looked ahead without saying a word.

"Aw, you're no fun," the biker said. "I'm gonna gun it the rest of the way."

"Hold it."

Pluto VIII went pale for a minute at the sharp command, but, in what was probably a show of false courage, he gave the grip starter a good twist. Uranium fuel sent pale flames spouting from the boosters, and the bike shot off in a cloud of dust. It stopped almost as quickly. The engine was still shuddering away, but the wheels were just kicking up sand. In the dazzling moonlight, his atomic-powered bike was not only refusing to budge an inch despite its five-thousand-horsepower output, it was actually sinking into the ground. "Dammit all," he hissed, "a sand viper!"

The creature in question was a colossal serpent that lived deep in the earth, and, although no one had ever seen the entire body of one, they were said to grow upwards of twenty miles long. Frighteningly enough, though the creatures were said to live their entire lives without ever moving a fraction of an inch, some believed they used high-frequency vibrations to create fragile layers of earth and sand in thousands of places on the surface so they might feed on those unfortunate enough to stumble into one of their traps. These layers moved relentlessly downward, becoming a kind of quicksand. Due to the startling motion the sands displayed, those who set foot into them would never make it out again. To get some idea of how tenacious the jaws of this dirt-and-sand trap were, one had only to watch how the five thousand horses in that atomic engine strained themselves to no avail. For all the bike's struggling, its wheels had already sunk halfway into the sand.

"Hey, don't just stand there watching, stone face. If you've got a drop of human blood in your veins, help me out here!" Pluto VIII shouted fervently. His words must've done the trick because D grabbed a thin coil of rope off the back of his saddle and dismounted. "If you screw this up, the rope'll get pulled down, too. So make your throw count," the man squawked, and then his eyes went wide. The gorgeous young man didn't throw him the rope. Keeping it in hand, he started to calmly walk into the quicksand. Pluto VIII opened his mouth to howl some new curse at the youth, but it just hung open—and for good reason.

The young man in black had started to stride elegantly over deadly jaws that would wolf down any creature they could find. His black raiment danced in the wind, the moonlight ricocheting off it as flecks of silver. He almost looked like the Grim Reaper coming in the guise of aid, but ready to wrap a black cord around the neck of those reaching out to him for succor.

The rope flew through the air. Excitedly grabbing hold of the end of it, Pluto VIII tied it around his bike's handlebars. The rest of the coiled rope still in hand, D went back to solid ground and climbed onto his cyborg horse without saying a word.

"Alright! Now on the count of—" Pluto never got to finish what he was saying as his bike was tugged forward. "Hey! Give me a second. Let me give it some gas, too," he started to say, but he only had a moment to tighten his grip on the throttle before the bike and its two riders were free of the living sands and its tires were resting once more on solid ground.

"Bucko, what the hell are you anyway?" Pluto VIII asked the mounted youth, with a shocked look on his face. "We'd be lucky to get away from a sand viper with a tractor pulling us, never mind a cyborg horse. And here you go and yank us out without even working up a sweat . . . I thought you was a mite too good-looking, but you're not human after all, are you?" Smacking his hands together, he exclaimed, "I've got it—you're a dhampir!"

D didn't move. His eternally cold gaze was fixed on the moonlit reaches of the darkness, as if seeking a safe path.

"But you don't have anything to worry about," the biker added. "My motto is 'Keep an open mind.' It don't matter if the folks around me have red skin or green—I don't discriminate. So long as they don't do wrong by yours truly, that is. Naturally, that includes dhampirs, too." Pluto VIII's voice had the ring of unquestionable sincerity to it.

Suddenly, without glancing at the biker who seemed ready to burst with the milk of human kindness, D asked in a low voice, "Are you ready?"

"For what?" Pluto VIII must've caught something in the Hunter's disinterested tone because his eyes went to D, then instantly swept around to the left and right, to the fore and rear. Aside from the piece of land the three of them were on, little black holes were forming all over the place. As sand coursed down into them the way it does into an antlion pit, the funnel-shaped holes quickly grew larger until one touched another, encircling the trio like the footprints of some unseen giant.

II

Son of a bitch . . . Don't seem like this freakin' sand viper aims to let us out of here alive," Pluto VIII said, the laughter strong in his voice. Sometimes a bit of cheer came to him in the midst of utter despair, but that had nothing to do with Pluto VIII's laugh, still full of confidence and hope.

But how on earth could they get themselves out of this mess? It didn't look like even D, with all his awesome skill, could get out of these preposterously large antlion pits. Especially since he wasn't alone. His traveling companion had a young woman strapped to his back, and, since she was suffering from extreme radiation poisoning, time was of the essence.

"Hey, what do we do?" Pluto VIII asked, looking extremely interested in the answer.

"Close your eyes and duck!" came the harsh reply.

Pluto VIII didn't have the faintest idea what was going on, but the instant he complied the whole world filled with white light. Under the pillar of light stretching down to the bottom of the colossal funnel, grains of sand grew super-hot, bubbled, and cooled almost instantly into a glassy plain reflecting the moon. The pillar of light silently stretched to the sky time and again, and, as D squinted ever so slightly at this mixing of light and darkness, his face was at times starkly lit, at other times deep in shadow. It seemed to go on for ages, but it couldn't have taken more than a few seconds. Aside from the dim, white depressions gleaming like water, the moonlit plain was just as it'd been before—deathly still.

"Looks like an atomic blast blew the hell out the sand viper holes—melted 'em and turned 'em to glass. Who the hell could've done that?" Pluto VIII asked, and then he once again followed D's gaze. He might've been well informed, but a gasp of wonder escaped from him nonetheless.

A black shadow that seemed both circular and oblong clung to the central part of the distant mountain range. It wasn't on the mountain's rocky walls. The shadowy shape was crossing the mountain peaks. Not only that, but, as it slowly moved forward, it was clearly coming lower as well. Taking the distance into consideration, it must've been moving at a speed of twelve or thirteen miles per hour at least. It was round, and about two miles in diameter.

"So, we have them to thank then?" Pluto VIII asked.

D gave a negligible nod. "Good thing there's still a mobile town around equipped with a Prometheus cannon. Incredible marksmanship, too. Our saviors got here right on schedule."

"Well, thank heaven for that. I just hope the mayor ain't the kind of guy who'll expect us to return the favor. Let's go," said the biker. "I don't feel like waiting around for the town to get here!"

The bike's boosters roared and the thud of iron-shod hooves on earth echoed across the plain. After they'd run at full speed for a good ten minutes, the huge black shape floated up over the crest of a hill before them like a cloud. The bottom was covered with spheres constructed of iron and wood, as well as with pipes. The white smoke erupting from the latter indicated that compressed air was one of the types of energy driving the cloud forward. And yet, how much thrust would be necessary just to move this thing an inch? After all, this massive structure that made the earth tremble as it came over the slope and slowly slid down it was a whole town. Even knowing that, even seeing it up close, it was no easy task to

comprehend something so awesome. The town must've covered more than two square miles. On top of a massive circular base some thirty feet high, buildings of wood, plastic, and iron were clustered together. Between them ran streets, some straight and orderly, others twisting and capricious. At the edge of the densely packed buildings there was a small park and a cluster of tombstones that marked the cemetery. Of course, in addition to the residential sector, there was everything you'd find in an ordinary village or town—a hospital, a sheriff's office, a jail, and a fire station. In the park, live trees swayed with the wind.

Startlingly enough, the base that supported this colossal establishment and was indispensable in its smooth movement hovered some three feet off the ground. That wasn't something just compressed-air jets or rocket engines could manage. No doubt power produced by the atomic reactor inside the base was run through a subatomic particle-converter and changed to antigravity energy. Still, to keep the structure a good three feet off the ground, there had to be some secret to the output of their atomic reactor or the capacity of their converters.

The base loomed blackly before the two men, and the mechanical whoosh blew closer and closer. A blinding light flashed down on the trio of travelers from a platform near the iron inlay on the top edge of the base. A voice boomed over the speakers. "What do you folks want?"

Pluto VIII pulled the microphone from his bike to his mouth and answered, "We're travelers. And we got an injured person here. We'd like to have a doctor take a look at 'er. Would you let us in?"

There was silence. The searchlight continued to shine on the pair. Well-concealed guns, no doubt, had them locked in their crosshairs. After a while, there was a reply. "No can do. We're not taking on any new blood. The town's population is already thirty percent over what our resources can support. Find yourselves another town or village. The closest one's twelve and a half miles from here—a place by the name of Hahiko."

"You've gotta be yanking my chain!" Pluto VIII growled, pounding a fist against his handlebars. "Who the hell's talking about twelve and a half miles?! Look, this girl I've got on my back's been doused real bad with radiation. She couldn't make it another hundred yards, let alone twelve and a half miles. What are you, the freaking Nobility?!"

"Nothing you say's gonna make any difference," the voice said coldly. "These orders come from the mayor. On top of that, the girl is part of the Knight family—Lori's her name. Two and a half months back they left town, so we're not about to let one of them back in now."

"I don't give a rat's ass about that. We got a girl in the prime of her life about to die. What, don't any of you have kids?"

The voice fell silent again. When another announcement rang out, it was a different person's voice. "We're set to roll," the new speaker said, "so clear the way!" And then, sounding somewhat agitated, he added, "Hey, young fellah—you wouldn't happen to be named D, would you?"

The youth nodded slightly.

"Oh, you should've said so in the first place. I'm the one who sent for you. Mayor Ming's the name. Just a second and we'll let you on board."

Machinery groaned, the iron door rose upward, and a boarding ramp started to glide out.

D said softly, "I've got some companions."

"Companions?!" Mayor Ming's voice quavered. "I'd always heard you were the most aloof, independent Hunter on earth. Just when did you get these companions?"

"Earlier."

"Earlier? You mean those two?"

"Do you see anyone else?" the Hunter asked.

"No—it's just . . . "

"I've fought side by side with them. That's the only reason I have. But if you have no business with me, I'll be on my way."

"W . . . wait a minute." The mayor's tone shifted from vacillating to determined. "We can't afford to lose you. I'll make a special exception for them. Come aboard."

The earth shook as the broad boarding-ramp hit the ground. Once the travelers were on, along with the bike and the cyborg horse, the ramp began to rise once again.

"The nerve of these people and their overblown escalator," Pluto VIII carped.

As soon as the ramp had retracted into the town's base, an iron door shut behind them and the two men found themselves in a vast chamber that reeked of oil. A number of armed men in the prime of life and a gray-haired old man stood there. The latter was more muscular in build than the men who surrounded him. Mayor Ming, no doubt. He may have had trouble walking, as he carried a steel cane in his right hand. "Glad you could make it," he said. "I'm Ming."

"Introductions can wait," Pluto VIII bellowed. "Where's the doctor?"

The mayor gave a nod, and two men stepped forward and unstrapped the girl—Lori—from the biker's back. "I imagine your companion's more interested in eating than hearing us talk business," the mayor said, signaling the other men with his eyes.

"Damn straight—you read my mind. Well, I'm off then, D. See you later."

When Pluto VIII had disappeared through a side door following his guides at his own leisurely pace, the mayor led D to a passage-way that continued up to the next level. The whistling of the wind seemed to know no end. All around them, ash-colored scenery rolled by. Forests and mountains. The town was moving across Innocent Prairie, the second of the Frontier's great plains. Whipping the Hunter's pitch-black cape and tossing his long, black hair, the wind blurred the wilds around them like a distant watercolor scene.

"How do you like the view?" Mayor Ming made a wave of one arm as if mowing down the far reaches of the plain. "Majestic, isn't it?" he said. Perhaps he'd taken the lack of expression on the young man staring off into the darkness as an expression of wonder. "The town maintains a cruising speed of twelve miles per hour. She can climb any mountain range or cliff, so long as it's less than a sixty-degree incline. Of course, we can only do that when we give the engines a blanket infusion of antigravity energy. This is how we always guarantee our five hundred residents a safe and comfortable journey."

"A comfortable journey, you say?" D muttered, but his words might not have reached the mayor's ears. "That's fine, as long as wherever you're headed is safe and comfortable, too. What do you want with me?"

The Hunter's hair flew in the wind that howled across the darkened sky. They were standing on an observation platform set at the very front of the town. If this had been a ship, it would've been the bow—or perhaps the prow. Jutting as it did from the top of the town's base, it seemed like it'd be the perfect spot to experience wind and rain and all the varied aspects of the changing seasons.

"Don't you care how that girl Lori's doing?" the mayor asked, ignoring D's inquiry.

"Stick to business."

"Hmm. A man who can slice a laser beam in two, who's discarded all human emotion . . . You're just like the stories make you out to be. I don't care how thick the Noble blood runs in you dhampirs, you could stand to act a tad more human."

D turned to leave.

"Come now. Don't go yet. Aren't you the hasty one," the mayor called, not seeming particularly overanxious. "There's only one reason anyone ever calls a Vampire Hunter—and that's for killing Nobility."

D turned back.

"When I let that man on two hundred years ago, I never in my wildest dreams would've thought something like this could happen," the mayor muttered. "That was the biggest mistake of my life."

D brushed his billowing hair back with his left hand.

"He was standing at the foot of the Great Northern Mountains, all alone. When we had him in the spotlight, he looked like the very darkness condensed. Now as a rule this town doesn't take on folks we just meet along the way, but it might've been the way he looked that stopped us dead in our tracks. There was a deep, dark look to his eyes. Come to think of it, he looked a lot like you."

The wind filled the sudden gap in conversation. After a pause, the mayor continued. "As soon as he was aboard, he came up here to the deck and looked out at the nocturnal wilds and rugged chain of mountains for the longest time. And then he calmly turned to me and said, 'Choose from the townsfolk five men and five women of surpassing strength and intellect, that they may join me in my travels.' Of course, I had to chuckle at that. At which point he laughed like thunder and said, 'Agree to my offer, and your people will know a thousand years of glory. Refuse, and this town will be cursed for all eternity to wander the deadly wilds,'" said the mayor, breaking off there. Pitch-black fatigue clung to his powerful and strangely smooth face. "Then he was gone. A touch of anxiety filled my heart, but nothing happened to the town after that. The next two hundred years weren't exactly one continuous stretch of peace and prosperity, but now I think I can safely say they were times of pure bliss. Now that the dark days are upon us. If this town is indeed under a curse as he decreed, we shall never be graced with glory or prosperity again."

Perhaps the reason the mayor had invited the Vampire Hunter up onto the deck was to show him the deadly wilds of their destiny.

"Come with me," Mayor Ming said. "I'll show you the real problem at hand."

A girl lay on a simple bed. Even without seeing her paraffin-pale skin or the wounds at the base of her throat, it was clear she was a victim of the Nobility. The most unsettling thing about her was her eyes—she had them trained on the ceiling, but they still had the spark of life.

"This is my daughter Laura. She's almost eighteen," said the mayor.

D didn't move, but remained looking down at the pale throat against the pillow.

"Three weeks ago she started acting strangely," said Mayor Ming. "I picked up on it when she said she thought she was coming down with a cold and started wearing a scarf. I never would've dreamed it could happen. It's just impossible we'd have a Noble in our town of all places."

"Has she been bitten again since then?"

At D's icy words, the distraught mayor nodded his head. "Twice. Both at night. We had one of our fighting men watching over her each time, but both times they were asleep before they knew it. Laura keeps losing more and more blood, but we've seen hide nor hair of the Nobility."

"You've done checks, haven't you?"

"Five times—and thorough ones at that. Everyone in town can walk in the light of day."

But D knew that such a test wasn't proof-positive that one of the townspeople wasn't a vampire. "We'll run another check later," D said, "but tonight I'll stay with her."

A shade of relief found its way into the mayor's steely expression. Though the man had lived more than two centuries, apparently, at heart, he was just like any other father. "I'd appreciate that. Can I get you anything?"

"I'm fine," D replied.

"If I may be so bold, could I say something?" The firm tone reminded the mayor and Hunter there was someone else present. A young physician stood by the door with his arms folded. Making no effort to conceal the anger in his face, he glared at D.

"Pardon me, Dr. Tsurugi. You have some objection to all this?" the mayor said, bowing to the young man who'd interrupted them. The doctor had been introduced to D when the mayor brought the Hunter to his daughter's room. He was a young circuit doctor who traveled from village to village out on the Frontier. Like D, he had black hair and dark eyes, and there didn't appear to be much difference in their ages. But, of course, as a dhampir D's age wasn't exactly clear, so external appearances were useless for comparisons.

The young physician shook his intelligent yet still somewhat innocent face from side to side. "No, I have no objection. Since there's nothing more I can do for her as a physician, I'll entrust the next step to this Hunter. However—"

"Yes?" said the mayor.

"I would like to keep watch over Ms. Laura with him. I realize I might sound out of line here, but I believe it's part of my duty as her physician."

Mayor Ming pensively tapped the handle of his cane against his forehead. While he probably considered the young physician's request perfectly natural, he also must've wished Dr. Tsurugi had never suggested such a troubling arrangement.

Before the mayor could turn to the Hunter, D replied, "If my opponent can't escape, there'll be a fight. I won't be able to keep you out of harm's way."

"I can look out for myself."

"Even if it means you might get bitten by one of them?" asked the Hunter.

Anyone who lived on the Frontier understood the implication of those words, and for a heartbeat the hot-blooded doctor's expression stiffened with fear, but then he replied firmly, "That's a chance I'm willing to take." His eyes seemed to blaze with intensity as he glared at D.

"Not a chance," D said, impassively.

"But, why the—I mean, why not? I said quite clearly I was prepared to—"

"If by some chance something were to happen to you, it would turn the whole town against me."

"But that's just . . . " Dr. Tsurugi started to say. His face was flushed with crimson anger, but he bit his lip and choked back any further contentions.

"Well, then, I'd like you both to step outside now. I have some questions for the girl," D said coolly, looking to the door. That was the signal for them to leave. There was something about the young man that could destroy any will to resist they still had.

As the mayor and Dr. Tsurugi turned to leave, the wooden door in front of them creaked open.

"Hey, how are you doing, tough guy?" someone said in a cheery voice. The face that poked into the room belonged to none other than John M. Brasselli Pluto VIII.

"How did you get here?" the mayor asked sharply.

"I, er . . . I'm terribly sorry, sir," said one of the townsfolk behind the biker—apparently a guard. "You wouldn't believe how stubborn this guy is, and he's strong as an ox."

"Don't have a fit now, old-timer," Pluto VIII said, smiling amiably. "I figured D'd probably be at your place. And it's not like there's anyone in town who doesn't know where the mayor lives. Anyhow—D, I found out how the girl's doing. That's what I came to tell you."

"I already told him some time ago," Dr. Tsurugi said with disdain. "He learned about her condition while you were busy eating."

"What the hell?! Am I the last one to know or something?!" Pluto VIII scratched wildly at a beard that looked as dense as the jungle when seen from the air. "Okay, no big deal. C'mon, D! Let's go pay her a visit."

"You do it."

As the gorgeous young man leaned over the bed just as indifferent as he was before, Pluto VIII asked him, "What gives, bucko? You risk your life saving a young lady and then you don't even wanna see if she's getting better? What, is the mayor's daughter so all-fired important?"

"This is business."

Pluto VIII had no way of knowing that it was nothing short of a miracle for D to answer such a contentious question. With an indignant look on his face matching that of the nearby physician, the biker pushed his way through the doorway. "Damn, I don't believe your nerve," he cursed. Spittle flew from his lips. "Do you *really* know how she's doing? She's got level three radiation poisoning to her speech center, and just as much damage to her sense of hearing to boot. And neither of them can be fixed. She's got some slight burns on her skin, too, but supplies of artificial skin are limited and, since it's not life-threatening, they'll leave her the way she is. How's that strike you? She's at the tender age where girls look up at the stars and weep, and now she's gonna have to carry the memory of watching her folks get eaten alive, her body is dotted with burns, and to top everything off she can't freakin' talk or hear no more."

More than the tragic details of what was essentially the utter ruin of that young woman, it was Pluto VIII's righteous indignation that made the mayor and Dr. Tsurugi lower their eyes.

D quietly replied, "I listened to what you had to say. Now get out."

III

Once the clamorous Pluto VIII had been pulled away from the room by the mayor and four guards, D looked down at Laura's face. Vacant as her gaze was, her eyes were still invested with a strange vitality, and they suddenly came into focus. The cohesive will she'd kept hidden tinged her eyes red. The will of a Noble. A breath howled out of her mouth. Like the corrupting winds gusting through the gates of Hell.

"What did you come here for?" she asked. Her eyes practically dripped venom as they stabbed back at D's. Laura's lips warped. Something could be seen glistening between her lips and overly active tongue. Canine teeth. Once again Laura said, "What are you here for?"

"Who defiled you?" asked D.

"Defiled me?" The girl's lips twisted into a grin. "To keep feeling the pleasure I've known, I wish I could be defiled night and day. What are you? I know you're not just an ordinary traveler. We don't get many folks around here who use words like defile."

"What time will he be here?"

"Well, now . . . Suppose you ask him yourself?" Her pleased expression suddenly stiffened. All the evil and rapture was stripped away like a thin veneer, and for a brief moment an innocent expression befitting a slumbering girl of eighteen skimmed across her face. Then, once again her features became as expressionless as paraffin. Dawn had come at last to the Great Northern Plains.

D raised his left hand and placed it on the young woman's forehead. "Exactly who or what attacked you?"

Consciousness returned to her cadaverous face. "I don't . . . know. Eyes, two red eyes . . . getting closer . . . but it's . . . "

"Is it someone from town?" asked D.

"I don't know . . . "

"When were you attacked?"

"Three weeks ago . . . in the park . . . " Laura answered slowly. "It was pitch black . . . Just those burning eyes . . . "

"When will he come next?"

"Oh . . . tonight . . . tonight . . . " Laura's body snapped tight, like a giant steel spring had suddenly formed inside her. The blankets flew off her with the force of it. She let out what sounded like a death rattle, the tongue lolled out of her mouth, and then her body began to rise in the most fascinating way. This paranormal phenomenon often occurred when a victim's dependency to the Nobility was pitted against some power bent on destroying that bond. Hunters frequently had an opportunity to observe this behavior, so D's expression didn't change a whit. But then, this young man's expression probably wouldn't show shock in a million years.

"Looks like that's all we'll be getting," said a hoarse voice that came from between the young woman's brow and the hand that rested against it. "The girl doesn't know anything aside from what she's told us. Guess we'll have to ask her little friend after all."

When the Hunter's hand was removed, Laura crashed back down onto the bed. Waiting until light as blue as water speared in through the window, D left the room. The mayor was waiting for him outside.

"Learned something in there, did you?" said Mayor Ming. He demonstrated the mentality of those who lived out on the Frontier by not asking the Hunter if he could save her or not.

The fact of the matter was, when a vampire with a victim in the works learned that a Hunter had come for him or her, they'd make themselves scarce unless the victim was especially dear to them. After that, it was all just a matter of time. The future of that victim might vary depending on how many times he or she'd been bitten, and how much blood had been taken. There were some who could go on to live a normal life even after five fateful visits to their bedroom—though they usually became social outcasts. But there were also some young ladies whose skin turned to pale paraffin from a single cursed kiss, and they'd lie in bed forever waiting for their caller to come again, never aging another day. And then one day a victim's gray-haired grandchildren and great-grandchildren would suddenly see her limbs shrivel like an old mummy's and know that somewhere out in the wide world the accursed Noble had finally met his fate. The question was, just how long would that take? How many living dead were still out there, sustained by nothing but moonlight, hiding in the corner of some rotting, dusty ruin, their kith and kin all long since dead? Time wasn't on the side of those who walked in the light of day.

"Tonight, we'll be having a visitor," D told the mayor.

"Oh, well that's just—"

"Is your daughter the only victim?"

The mayor nodded. "So far. But as long as whoever did this is still out there, that number could swell until it includes every one of us."

"I'd like you to prepare something for me," D said as he looked to the blue sky beyond the window.

"Just name it. If it's a room you need, we've already prepared your accommodations."

"No, I'd like a map of your town and data on all the residents," said D. "Also, I need to know everywhere the town has gone since it started its journey, and what destinations are set for the future."

"Understood," said the mayor.

"Where will my quarters be?"

"I'll show you the way."

"No need to do that," the Hunter replied.

"It's a single family house near the park. A bit old, perhaps, but it's made of wood. It's located . . ." After the mayor finished relating the directions, he pushed down on the grip of his cane with both hands and muttered, "It'd be nice if we could get this all settled tonight."

"Where was your daughter attacked?" D asked.

"In a vacant house over by the park. Didn't find anything there when we checked it out, though. It's not far from the house we have for you, either."

D asked for the location, and the mayor gave it to him.

Then D went outside. The wind had died down. Only its whistling remained. There must've been a device somewhere in town for projecting a shield over the entire structure. The town's defenses against the harsh forces of nature were indeed perfect. Blue light made the Hunter stand out starkly as he went down the street. The shadow he cast on the ground was faint. That was a dhampir's lot. There was no sign of the living in the residential sector. For the tranquil hours of night, people became like breathing corpses.

Up ahead, the Hunter could see a tiny point of light. A bit of warmth beckoning to the dawn's first light. A hospital. D walked past it without saying a word. He didn't seem to be looking at the signs that marked each street. His pace was like the wind.

After about twenty minutes he was out of the residential section, and he stopped just as the trees of the park came into view. To his right was a row of half-cylindrical buildings—one of them was his destination. That was where young Laura had been attacked. The mayor had told him all of the buildings were vacant. At first, that'd only been true for the building in question, but, after the incident involving Laura, the families living nearby had requested other quarters and moved out. Dilapidation was already creeping up on the structures.

The house on the end was the only one shut tight by poles and locks. The fact that it'd been sealed with heavy poles instead of ordinary planks made it clear how panicked the people were. And there were five locks on the door—all electronic.

D reached for the locks. The pendant at his breast gave off a blue light, and, at the mere touch of his pale fingertips, the locks dropped to his feet. His fingers closed on the poles, which had been fixed in a gigantic X. The poles of unmilled wood were over eight inches in diameter and had been riveted in place. D's hand wouldn't wrap even halfway around one. It didn't look like there'd be any way for him to get a good grip on them. But his fingertips sank into the bark. His left hand tore both poles free with one tug.

Pushing his way past a door that'd lost its paint in the same crisscrossing shape, D headed inside. A stench pervaded the place. It was the kind of stink that called to mind colors—colors beyond counting. And each of them painted its own repulsive image. As if something ominous beyond telling was drifting through the dilapidated house.

Though the windows were all boarded up, D casually advanced down the dark hallway, coming to the room where they'd found Laura. As the mayor had said, they'd performed an exhaustive search, and anything that wasn't nailed down had been taken out of the room. There were no tables, chairs, or doors here. D's unconcerned eyes moved ever so slightly as he stood in the center of the room.

He stepped out into the hall without making a sound. At the end of another hall that ran perpendicular to the first he could see the door to the next room. A shadow tumbled through the doorway. It was like a stain of indeterminate shape. Its contours shifted like seaweed underwater, and the center of it eddied. Then it stood up. A pair of legs were visible. A head and torso were vaguely discernible. It was a human wrapped in some kind of protective membrane. What on earth was it doing here?

D advanced slowly.

The stain didn't move. Its hands and feet changed shape from one moment to the next, yet their respective functions remained clear.

"What are you?" D asked softly. Though his tone was quiet, it had a ring to it that made it clear his questions weren't to be left unanswered, much less ignored. "What are you doing here? Answer me."

Swaying, the stain charged at him. It was a narrow hallway. D had no way of avoiding it. His right hand went for the longsword on his back—and dead ahead of him, his foe waved its arm. A black disk zipped toward D's face.

Narrowly ducking his head, D drew his longsword. Seeming to have some special insight into the situation, the Hunter didn't use his unsheathed weapon to parry the disk, but slashed with the blade from ground to sky. His foe had already halted its charge, and now a terrific white light flashed through its crotch. From the bottom up, his foe was bisected. And yet, aside from a slight ripple that ran through its whole body, the shifting shadow was unchanged. An indescribable sound echoed behind it. Regardless, D advanced.

Without making a sound, the shadow backed against the wall. It certainly seemed just like a real shadow, because its clearly three-dimensional form abruptly lost its depth and became perfectly flat before being completely and silently absorbed by the wall. D stood before the wall without saying a word. The gray surface of the tensile plastic was glowing faintly. That was the aftereffect of molecular intangibility—the ability to pass through walls without resistance. The process of altering cellular structure and passing through the molecules of some barrier caused subtle changes in radioactive isotopes. That same ability had probably allowed the shadow to evade the blow from D's sword.

Doing an about-face, D ran his eyes across either side of the hallway. The disk had vanished. There were no signs it'd hit anything, either.

D pushed open the same door the shadow had come from. It appeared to be a laboratory that'd been sealed in faint darkness. The walls were covered with all sorts of medicines, and the lab table bolted to the floor was covered with burn marks and was heavily discolored by stains. He noticed signs that some sort of mechanical device had been removed.

D came to a halt in the center of the room. There were shields over the windows. What kind of experiments had been performed here in the darkness, sealed away from the light? There was something extremely tragic about the place.

This was where the intruder had come from. Had it been living in here? Or had it slipped in before D arrived, searching for something? Probably the latter. In which case, it would be relatively easy to discover who it was. Five hundred people lived in this town. Finding the intruder among that many people wouldn't be impossible.

D went outside. There was something in this house. But he couldn't put his finger on what exactly it was. The sunlight gracing the world grew whiter. D came to a halt at the door. A black cloud was moving down the street. A mass of people. A mob. It almost looked like every person in town was there. The intense hostility and fear in their eyes made it plain they were fully aware of D's true nature.

D calmly made his way to the street. A black wall of a man suddenly loomed before him. He must've been about six foot eight and weighed around three hundred and thirty pounds. The giant had pectorals so wide and thick they looked like scales off a greater fire dragon. Leaving about three feet between them, D looked up at the man.

"Hey—you're a dhampir, ain't you?" The giant's deep voice was soaked with vermilion menace.

D didn't answer him.

Something flowed across the man's features like water. A frightened hue. He'd looked into D's eyes. Ten seconds or so passed before he managed to squeeze out another word. "Seeing as how the mayor called you to his house, there ain't much we can do about you. But this here's a town for clean-living folk. We don't want no Noble half-breed hanging around, okay?"

The heads of those around him moved in unison. Nodding their agreement. There were men and women there, and even children.

"There's Nobility here. Or someone who serves them," D said softly. "The next family attacked might be yours."

"If it comes to that, we'll take care of it ourselves," said the giant. "We don't need no help from the Nobility's side."

Nodding faintly, D took a step. That alone was enough to part the fearful crowd. The giant and the others moved back like the outgoing tide.

"Wait just a damn minute!" Embarrassed perhaps to be afraid, the giant unleashed a tone that had a fierceness born of hysteria. "I'm gonna pound the shit out of you now, buster."

While he said this, the giant slipped on a pair of black leather gloves. The backs of them looked like plain leather, but the palms

were covered with thin, flexible metal fibers. When the giant
smacked his hands together, it set off clusters of purple sparks that
stretched out like coral branches. People backed away speechless.
Electromagnetic gloves like these were used by huntsmen. The
highest setting on them was fifty thousand volts. Capable of killing
a mid-sized fire dragon, they were lethal weapons to be sure.

"What are you, scumbag—half human? Or is it a third?" the
giant sneered. "Whatever the hell it is, you're just lucky you're sort
of like us. Now say your prayers that the only part of you I burn to
a crisp is your filthy Noble blood." Purple sparks dyed his rampaging
self-confidence a grotesque hue.

D started to walk away, oblivious to the giant's threats. The
giant ran at him, right hand raised and ready for action. D's
movements and his expression were unchanged. Like shadows
that'd never known the light.

A sharp glint of light burned through the air. The giant shook
his hand in pain. Sparks leapt wildly from his palm, and then a slim
scalpel fell to the ground.

"What the hell are you doing?!" The giant's enraged outburst
went past D and straight on down the street. Coming toward them
with determined strides, his lab coat crisp and white, was none other
than Dr. Tsurugi. "Oh, it's you, Doc," the big man said. "What
the hell are you trying to do?" Though he tried his best to sound
threatening, there was no doubt the giant had the recognizable
threat of the physician's scalpel-throwing to thank for the slight
tremble in his voice.

Coming to a stop in front of the crowd, Dr. Tsurugi said sharply,
"Would you knock it off? This man is a guest of the mayor. Instead
of trying to chase him off, you should be working with him to find
the Nobility. Mr. Berg!" An elderly man, older than anyone else
there, seemed shaken by the physician's call. "You were right here—
why didn't you put a stop to this? If we lose our Hunter, it stands
to reason the Nobility will remain at large. As you'll recall, all *our*
searches have ended in failure."

"I, er . . . yeah, I thought so, too. It's just . . . " Berg stammered ashamedly. "Well, if he was a regular Hunter it'd be one thing. But him being a dhampir and all, I knew they wouldn't go for it. You know, the women and children been scared stiff since they heard the rumors he was here."

"And they can get by with just a good scare—a Noble will do far worse to them, I assure you," Dr. Tsurugi said grimly.

"B . . . but, Doc," a middle-aged woman cradling a baby stammered, "they say dhampirs do it, too. I hear when they're thirsty, they drink the blood of people they're working for . . . "

"Damned if that ain't the truth," the giant bellowed. "See, it ain't like we got no grounds for complaining. The whole damn town may be on the move, but information still gets in. Y'all remember what happened in Peamond, right?"

That was the name of a village where half the townsfolk had died of blood loss in a single night. Descending from the Nobility, dhampirs had a will of iron, but on occasion their spirit could succumb to the sweet siren call of blood. The man who'd been hired in Peamond found the black bonds of blood he'd tried so long to keep in check stirred anew by the beauty of the mayor's daughter, and then the Hunter himself became one of those he hunted. Before the inhabitants of the village got together and held him down long enough to drive a stake through his heart, the toll of victims had reached twenty-four.

"That's the grandfather of all exceptions." There was no vacillation whatsoever in Dr. Tsurugi's tone. "I happen to have the latest statistics. The proportion of dhampirs who've caused that sort of tragedy while on the job is no more than one twenty-thousandth of a percent."

"And what proof do we have that this ain't gonna be one of those cases?!" the giant shouted. "We sure as hell don't wanna wind up that fucking one twenty-thousandth of a percent. Ain't that right, folks?"

A number of voices rose in agreement.

"Come to think of it, Doc, you ain't from around here, neither. What's the story? You covering for him because you outsiders gotta stick together or something? I bet that's it—the two of you dirty dogs been in cahoots all along, ain't you?!"

All expression faded from Dr. Tsurugi's face. He stepped forward, saying, "You wanna do this with those gloves on? Or are you gonna take them off?"

The giant face twisted. And formed a smile. "Oh, this'll be good," he said, switching off the gloves and pulling them from his hands. From the expression on his face, you'd think he was the luckiest man on earth. The way the physician had nailed him with a scalpel earlier was pretty impressive, but aside from that he was only about five foot eight and tipped the scales at around a hundred and thirty-five pounds. The giant had strangled a bear before, so, when it came down to bare-knuckle brawling, he was supremely confident in his powerful arms.

"You sure you wanna do that, Conroy?" Berg asked, hustling in front of the giant to stop him. "What do you reckon they'll do to you if you bust up our doctor? You won't get no slap on the wrist, that's for damn sure!"

"So what—they'll give me a few lashes and shock me a couple of times? Hell, I'm used to it. Tell you what—I'll leave the doc's head and hands in one piece when I bust him up." Roughly shoving Berg out of the way, the giant stepped forward.

As the young physician also took a step forward, D called out from behind him, "Why don't you call it quits? This started out as my fight, after all."

"Well, it's mine now, so I'll thank you to just stand back and watch."

The air whistled. It could've been Conroy letting out his breath, or the whine of his punch ripping through the wind. Dr. Tsurugi jumped to the side to dodge a right hook as big and hard as a rock. As if the breeze from the punch had whisked him away. The young physician had both hands up in front of his chest in lightly clenched fists. How many of the people there noticed the calluses covering his knuckles, though? Narrowly avoiding the uppercut the giant threw as his second punch, Dr. Tsurugi let his left hand race into action. The path it traveled was a straight line.

To Conroy, it looked like everything past the physician's wrist had vanished. He felt three quick impacts on his solar plexus. The first two punches he took in stride, but the third one did the trick. He tried to exhale, but his wind caught in his throat. The physician's blows had a power behind them one would never imagine from his unassuming frame.

A bolt of beige lightning shot out at the giant's wobbling legs. No one there had ever seen such footwork. The physician's leg limned an elegant arc that struck the back of Conroy's knee, and the giant flopped to the ground with an earthshaking thud. Straight, thrusting punches from the waist and circular kicks—there'd been no hesitation in the chain of mysterious attacks, and how powerful they were soon became apparent as Conroy quickly started to get back up. As soon as the giant tried to put any weight on his left knee, he howled in pain and fell on his side.

"Probably won't be able to stand for the rest of the day," the young physician said, looking around at the chalk-white faces of the people as if nothing had happened. "Just goes to show it doesn't pay to go around whipping up mobs. All of you move along now. Back to your homes."

"Yeah, but, Doc," a man with a long, gourd-shaped face said as he pointed to Conroy, "who's gonna see to his wounds?"

"I'll have a look at him," Dr. Tsurugi said with resignation. "Bring him by the hospital some time. Just don't do it for about three days or so. Looks like it'll take him that long to cool down. But from here on out, there's a damn good chance I'll refuse to treat anyone who raises a hand to the Hunter here, so keep that in mind. Okay, move along now." After he'd seen to it that the people dispersed and Conroy had been carried away, Dr. Tsurugi turned to face D.

"That's a remarkable skill you have," the Hunter said. "I recall seeing it in the East a long time ago. What is it?"

"It's called karate. My grandfather taught it to me. But I'm surprised you'd put up with so much provocation."

"I didn't have to. You put an end to it. Maybe you did it to keep me from having to hurt any of the locals . . . Whatever the reason, you helped me out."

"No, I didn't." There was mysterious light in the physician's eyes as he shook his head. While you couldn't really call it amity, it wasn't hostility or enmity, either. You might call it a kind of tenacity.

And then D asked him, "Have we met somewhere before?"

"No, never," the physician said, shaking his head. "As I told you, I'm a circuit doctor. In my rounds out on the Frontier, I've heard quite a few stories about you."

The physician looked like he had more to say, but D interrupted him, asking, "Who used to live in that abandoned house?"

The physician's eyes went wide. "You mean to tell me you didn't know before you went in? The house belongs to Lori Knight—the girl you rescued."

Destination Unknown

CHAPTER 2

I

The girl was sitting up in bed. She looked like a snow-capped doll—the plaster for removing radioisotopes that covered her limbs was called snow parts. Glowing faintly in the evening from the radiation it'd drawn from her body, it hid the soul-chilling tragedy that'd befallen her beneath the beauty of new-fallen snow.

"There's no immediate threat to her life. I believe you heard all about her condition from Pluto VIII."

D met the physician's words with silence. The girl—Lori—was reflected in the Hunter's eyes, but what deeper emotions the sight of her stirred in D's psyche even Dr. Tsurugi couldn't tell. Or maybe it didn't stir anything at all. The physician thought that'd be entirely appropriate for the young man.

They were in one of the rooms in the hospital that stood near the center of the residential sector. Dr. Tsurugi and a middle-aged nurse lived there and treated every imaginable ailment, dealing with everything from the common cold to installing cyborg parts. His skill at being able to handle such a wide range of health problems made him a qualified, and accomplished, circuit doctor.

"Could I put some questions to her in writing?"

D's query put Dr. Tsurugi's head at a troubled tilt. "Perhaps for a short time," he said reluctantly. "It's just . . ."

D waited for his explanation.

"I'd like you to refrain from asking her any questions that may likely prove shocking. We're dealing with a young lady who's been seriously wounded both physically and psychologically. She's already well aware of what the future holds for her."

"How old is she?"

"Seventeen."

D nodded.

The physician looked rather concerned, but he soon walked over to Lori's bedside, took the memo pad and electromagnetic pen from beside her pillow, and jotted something down. An introduction for D, no doubt. Her white shoulders shook a bit, her downturned face shifted slightly toward D—then stopped. D watched expressionlessly as her face turned down again and her lily-white fingers took the electromagnetic pen from the physician. The pen moved with short, powerful strokes. Like it was fighting something off. Tearing off the page, the physician stood up straight and handed the message to D. In beautiful, precise penmanship it read, *Thank you so much.*

Returning the sheet to the physician, D settled himself into the chair beside Lori's bed without saying a word. The blue eyes peeking out from under her various white wrappings suddenly opened wide. The girl turned her face away. Quickly bringing it back, she cast her gaze downward. From her reaction, she apparently recognized D.

The physician got another pen and notepad and handed them to D. The Hunter's hand quickly went into action. *There's someone in your house,* he wrote. *Were there any strange occurrences there before?*

Lori stared at the page he'd given her. And continued to do so for a long time. It seemed like nearly ten minutes passed before she shook her head from side to side.

Once again D's hand scrawled a few words. *Do you know what your father's experiments involved?*

Again, she shook her head.

D readied his pen once more.

Lori shook her head. Over and over she shook it. Her shoulders began to quake, too. Bits of healing plaster fell from her like snowflakes. Dr. Tsurugi held her shoulders steady. Still, Lori tried to go on shaking her head.

"Kindly leave. Hurry!" the physician said to D. The door swung open and the nurse rushed in.

Getting to his feet, D asked, "Where's Pluto VIII staying?"

"As I recall, he's in P9 in the special residential district. It's right by the law enforcement bureau," the physician called out, but his words merely echoed off the closed door and died away.

†

Exiting the hospital, D walked down the street. Despite the sudden madness they'd witnessed in Lori, his eyes were as cold and clear as ever. Any human emotion would've seemed like a blemish when it showed in the young man's eyes.

Though plenty of people were coming and going on the street, the path directly ahead of D was completely unobstructed. Every last person in his way stepped aside. They didn't do this out of the superstitious, ingrained distaste they had for those who dwelled outside their society, but because of the young man's good looks and the aura about him. Everyone knew. They also knew that not everyone out on the street was necessarily human.

And yet, there was a hint of intoxication in the eyes of all as they gazed at D. His gorgeous features made them shudder with something other than fear, and not only the women but even the men felt a sort of sexual excitement when they saw him. Most of the people wore work clothes and carried farm implements. Working the earth wasn't quite the same in a sector of a moving town, but people went about the business of living as best they could. They labored. On the far side of the park lay farms and fields, as well as a sprawling industrial sector.

D soon found the law enforcement bureau. Despite the grandiose name, it was no different from the sheriff's office you'd find in any town this size. The group of blue buildings across the street made up the special residential district. A pair of three-story buildings that looked like hotels—that was all there was to the district. As D came to the door, a cheerful voice shouted to him from across the street. On turning, the Hunter found Pluto VIII trotting his way. Both his hands were covered by a riot of colors—flowers.

"Hey, what are you doing, stud?" The biker wore a personable smile that made his hostility back at the mayor's house seem long forgotten. Once he'd reached D, he looked all around them. "They're mighty unfriendly in this town," he groused. "I heard there ain't a single florist anywhere. Someone said there was a flower garden, so I went to have a look-see, and they tell me out there they don't sell to outsiders. Well, that ain't so rare in itself, but I tell 'em, 'Dammit, I wanna take them to a sick friend,' and still they wouldn't give me the okay." He was truly indignant about this. Foam flying from his mouth, he added, "Hell, I told 'em the flowers were for Lori. I say, 'She used to live here just like the rest of you, right? I don't care if her family decided to leave; it ain't like she came back here because she wanted to. She lost her mother and father, and got hurt real bad herself, and only came back to try and save her life.' Son of a bitch—they still told me I couldn't have 'em. Said that once you leave town, you're an outsider."

To his snarling companion, D said softly, "So, how did you get those flowers then?"

"Well, er—you know. Anyway, I was pretty pissed off at the time."

"That's not exactly new territory for you, though."

"Yeah, you could say that," Pluto VIII confessed easily. It was frightening how quickly his mood could change. "Oh, well, not much I can do now. Anyway—did you have business with me?"

"I want to ask you something."

"Is that a fact? Well, let's not stand around here jawing. There's a bar around the corner. What do you say to having a drink while we talk?" Laughing, he added, "Don't think they serve human blood, though." Knowing exactly who he was saying this to, his joke might've had deadly repercussions, but D didn't seem to mind. He followed Pluto VIII.

†

The bar was packed. Work in town must've been done in shifts. As the two of them entered, all chatter in the watering hole stopped dead. The eyes of the bartender and the men around the various tables focused on the pair.

"Excuse me! Coming through! Pardon me!" Pluto VIII called out amiably as they slipped between the crowded tables, finally seating themselves at an empty one in the back. In a terribly gruff voice he shouted, "Hey, I'd like a bitter beer. That, and a—" Turning to D, he asked in a completely baffled manner, "What'll you have?"

"Nothing."

"Dope, you can't just walk into a bar and order nothing— you're a nuisance." Yelling, "He'll have the same," to the bartender, Pluto VIII turned to D again. "So, what's this business you have with me?"

"I went into a certain house earlier," D said. "There was someone strange inside. Wasn't you, was it?"

"What do you mean?"

"I don't think anyone from town would be rooting through the house at this late date. And the only ones here from somewhere else are you and me."

Pluto VIII leaned back and laughed heartily. Those seated around them flinched and gave him startled looks. "Hate to disappoint you, but it wasn't me. Hell, even if it was me, you think I'd just come right out and say so?"

"Why are you here? Seems someone like you would be better off leaving town."

"I'd tend to agree with you," Pluto VIII conceded easily. "But it ain't that simple. Why, compared to the world down there, this place is like heaven. If you got money to spend, you can buy just about anything, and you can get by without messing around with any of the Nobility's deadly little pals. I tell you, I plan to stick around until they toss me out on my ear."

"You couldn't buy flowers," D reminded him.

"Yeah, but that don't change much." But, just as his confident smile spread across his gruff face, a number of people piled in through the bar door. A gray-haired crone was at the fore, and behind her three powerful-looking young men. All four were pale with anger.

D's eyes dropped to the bouquet on the table, and he said, "You stole those, didn't you?"

"No, I'm renting them, you big dope. I just didn't leave a deposit for them."

The whole bar started to buzz with chatter, and a bunch of people gathered around D and Pluto VIII's table. "There he is. There's the no-good flower thief. I'm sure of it," the crone shrieked, her bony finger aimed at Pluto VIII's face.

"Now that ain't a very nice thing to say," Pluto VIII said, knitting his brow. "I'm just borrowing these to take 'em to a sick friend, okay? What could make a flower happier than that?"

"The hell you say!" The crone's hairline and the corners of her eyes rose with her tone. "Do you have any idea how much back-breaking toil it takes to grow a single flower in this town? Of course you don't! You're a dirty, rotten thief!"

"He sure is," another person surrounding the table chimed in. "And thieves gotta pay a price. Let's step outside."

"Nothing doing," Pluto VIII laughed mockingly. "What'll you do if I don't go?"

"Then we'll have no choice but to use force."

The biker's confident laughter flew in the faces of the tense men. "Do you folks know who the hell I am? I'm the one and only John M. Brasselli Pluto VIII, known far and wide across the Frontier."

Silence.

"What, you bastards never heard of me?" Pluto VIII said with a scowl. "Well, at any rate, I bet you know my friend here. The most handsome cuss on the Frontier, a first-rate slayer of Nobility, an apostle of the dream demons, and all the beauty of the darkness in human form—I give you the Vampire Hunter D!"

Every face around them went pale. Even those of the men in the very back of the bar.

"Hell of a reputation he's got, eh?" Pluto VIII chortled. Looking around at the men who were now still and pale as corpses, he asked, "Still want us to step outside? My buddy can split a laser beam in two."

"For your information, this doesn't concern me at all," said D, his gazed fixed on the same spot on the table the whole time.

"What do you mean?" Pluto VIII said, bugging his eyes. "Oh, you're cold-blooded. Aren't we buddies? Don't listen to him, guys," Pluto VIII laughed. "He was only joking."

"Go outside if you want. But leave me out of this," said the Hunter.

"I don't believe you!" Pluto VIII rose indignantly. "Did you forget about the beer I just bought you?"

"Sorry, sir, about that," someone called from behind the bar, "we just ran out of your beer."

"God damn it all, this just ain't my day!" Pluto VIII cursed.

"Quit your bellyaching and step outside already," said one of the men surrounding him. "Stealing flowers is stealing all the same, and a thief's still gotta pay the price."

"Oh, really? And what did you have in mind?"

"A thousand lashes with the electron whip, or thirty days hard labor."

"Don't care much for either. Well, I'll go out with you anyway."
Giving D a look that could kill, Pluto VIII didn't seem terribly
afraid as he followed the men out. Still, it wasn't the fight headed
outside that every eye in the place was following—their eyes were
riveted to the handsome young man who remained at the table.

Four men escorted Pluto VIII outside. Two of them were in
their thirties, while the other two were younger. They must've
been around twenty years old. As was normal for laborers on the
Frontier, the mass of their muscles was evident even through their
rough apparel. Every one of them stood over six feet tall. Pluto VIII,
on the other hand, was five foot four. The biker was just as big
through the chest and shoulders, but, in a bare-knuckle brawl,
he'd be at an overwhelming disadvantage.

Snapping his fingers, Pluto VIII asked, "Okay, who wants to
be first?"

"Don't go looking to get yourself hurt any worse than need
be," said the man who seemed to be their leader. "Just come along
quietly to the law enforcement bureau and take your pick of the
two punishments. Then this'll all be over."

Pluto VIII chuckled. "Not a chance." His face brimmed with
self-confidence. Beneath the beard that hid his mouth, his deep
red tongue was licking his lips. "If there's one thing I can't stand,
it's assholes who get all tough when the numbers are on their side.
See, I'm more of a loner. So don't just stand there acting scary.
Hurry up and come get a piece of me!"

Even before he had time to realize the last bit had been a
challenge, the young man on the left took a swing at Pluto VIII.
He didn't say a word, didn't even exhale. He must've been a first-
rate brawler. Just as the two figures were about to make contact, Pluto
VIII backed away without moving a muscle. Still swinging his right
hand down as hard as he could, the young man had no time to
compensate and hit the ground shoulder first. What the hell
happened? The perfect timing of the biker's defense against the
attack almost made it look like the two of them were in collusion.

"Okay, next!" said the broadly smirking Pluto VIII. He didn't look the least bit perturbed. In fact, he seemed to be enjoying the brawl. Whatever weird trick he had up his sleeve, it made Dr. Tsurugi's martial arts seem commonplace by comparison.

The remaining trio of opponents were united by disquiet.

"What's the problem? I'll take the three of you at once. Look . . . " Both hands hanging down by his sides so he was left wide open, Pluto VIII lifted his chin to them as if begging them to punch it.

Howling curses, the two men in their thirties rushed him—one from the front, the other from behind. Trusting the abdominal muscles they'd hardened with a deep breath to protect them from any odd attack by Pluto VIII, the men had their arms spread wide to smash the little guy like a bug. It was a plan of attack that made it plain they had little regard for someone of his small stature. In a moment it became clear that was a mistake. As the two men came together to crush him, there was no trace of Pluto VIII there, and, the instant his form came back to earth some ten feet away, his massive assailants fell face first with a force that shook the ground. What the diminutive man had accomplished in this battle in the chill sunlight was nothing short of miraculous.

Nimbly, Pluto VIII turned around. The face of the one young adversary who remained was right before him. And it was more bloodless now than when he'd heard D's name mentioned before. "You coming to get some? How 'bout it, sonny?"

The only reply the young man had for that affable query was a dash in the opposite direction.

Watching the young tough run away without so much as a glance behind him, Pluto VIII's gaze was unexpectedly warm, and then his eyes shifted to the entrance to the bar. "What do you think of that? Am I faster than that sword of yours?" His tone was so steeped in self-confidence it made the sunlight pale by comparison, but D's only reply was a dark silence. "Well, then, I'm off to see a certain little lady next. You coming with me?"

Giving no answer, D turned away.

"Buddy, I don't care how damn good-looking you are, you gotta get a bit more sociable. I tell you, women these days are interested in what's inside a man." Cackling in a way that made it clear he was pleased with himself, even Pluto VIII couldn't be sure if his words had reached the black-clad figure whose back was now dwindling in the distance.

II

A few minutes later, Mayor Ming was greeting a visitor in black. "Why didn't you tell me about the house?"

The mayor recoiled from the serene tone in spite of himself. "What house?"

"Where they found your daughter. It seems it was the home of the girl who's in the hospital—Lori."

"That's right," the mayor said casually. "I didn't divulge that particular information because I didn't think it particularly vital. Did something happen?"

"I don't know exactly what happened, but someone was in there. I believe they were looking for something."

"What kind of character was it?" The mayor's eyes glittered with curiosity.

"There's no point getting into it. Have any of the townspeople shown any particular interest in that house?"

"Can't see how they could. The place is supposed to be locked up tight as a drum."

"Do you know of anyone in town with a talent for molecular intangibility?" asked D.

The mayor didn't answer.

"What was Lori Knight's family researching there?"

"He was merely . . . " the mayor began to say, but then he grew silent. A thin breath whispered from his lips. "For the longest time the Knights' experiments were the source of some concern for folks around town. Not their results, per se. It was simply that no one could grasp what they might be doing in there. As you're no doubt aware, in a town like this it's impossible to try and do anything without somebody finding out about it. At times, individual egos have been known to endanger the way of life for entire communities. I personally called on them more than a few times, but Franz—the girl's father—always maintained they were simple experiments in chemistry."

The mayor's face wore a heavy shade of fatigue. Saying not a word, D continued gazing out the window. As far as the eye could see, the brown plains bent away from them. The town's cruising speed, it seemed, was far from leisurely.

"If only I'd taken notice sooner . . ." the mayor continued. His voice was leaden. "Mr. and Mrs. Knight were the town's foremost chemists. It was only Mr. Knight's intellect that saved us from famine fifteen years back, or averted the thunder-beast attacks in the nick of time a mere four years ago. If not for him, a good seventy percent of the town would've gone to their reward. I thought we could overlook their somewhat unconventional hobby, and the townsfolk seemed to feel the same way. That was a mistake. And then one day, he suddenly decided to leave town . . . Yes, it was just about two months ago. I tried my best to dissuade him, but his resolve was strong as steel. I can still recall the look on his face. He looked like flames were ready to shoot out of his eyes. I suppose whatever he discovered here in town could've served him quite well in a life in the accursed world below. He could've very easily come up with something useful like that. And I had no choice but to let them off. Of course, I didn't neglect to make it perfectly clear they'd never again be allowed back in town. And that's all there was to it."

"I don't think it was," D said, as if conversing with the wind. "There was something in their house that bordered on utter ruin. Anyone would notice it. Where did you dispose of the things that were in the house?"

"There wasn't anything like that," the mayor said, fairly spitting the words. "The only really unsettling stuff was some odd-looking bottles of medicine and two or three contraptions it looked like he'd thrown together, and we wasted no time in destroying those. But the rest of the drugs and machinery were sent over to other labs or factories that could make use of them. There wasn't anything out of the ordinary at all."

"Who did the actual work?"

"Folks from all over town pitched in. Just check the names and you'll see."

"You mean to tell me you weren't involved?"

The mayor shook his head. "No. I give the orders around here. I was right there when it came time to board the place up."

D said nothing, but gazed at the mayor. His eyes were dark beyond imagining, and clearer than words could say. "I'll need a list of everyone involved in the project. I want to ask them about something."

"Why? Do you think I'm lying?" the mayor asked, not seeming the least bit angry.

"Anyone can lie," D replied.

"I suppose you've got a point there. Just give me a second. I'll make you a copy."

The mayor used the intercom on his desk to give the command to the listing computer, and in fewer than five seconds the mayor handed D a sheet of paper. The names and addresses of nearly twenty men were recorded on the list. Putting the paper in his coat pocket, D went back outside without making a sound.

†

The old room felt dirty. Aside from the industrial facilities, this place had more working machinery than anyplace else in the whole town, and after nuclear energy had been produced the waste was promptly processed and dispelled as

a harmless dust. Despite that, the room did indeed look somewhat
soot-stained.

A black figure crept over to the control panel that regulated
the trio of nuclear reactors. Because this section provided energy
for all the town's needs, it was protected by three Dewar walls each
six feet thick. All activity in the building was monitored by the
computer. Nevertheless, the shadowy figure stood suspiciously before
the controls, unnoticed by the electronic eyes and unrecorded in
their memories. A black hand entirely befitting the dark figure
reached out and began flicking off lights on the panel—something
that never should've been allowed.

†

In the depths of the swirling chaos, red spots began to form.
A few of these spots quickly fused into one, and from a spot it
grew to a stain, and from the stain a net formed. Within the scarlet
was her father's face. His expression was oddly calm. Blue light
danced about him. The light was as bright as lightning, but at
the same time it also looked somewhat like coral. Her father looked
up from the table. Several seconds later, an elated hue spread across
his emaciated features. Her father's lips moved. "I've done it," he
said. "I've finally done it."

The next thing she knew, her mother and father were wandering
about in the wilderness. In the distance, the wind howled. It was a
cold wind, as chilly as a fog. On the desolate plain before her there
was nothing to see but clouds and sky. The clouds eddied, and the
wind alone blew against her. And then that wind formed a face by
her. One she felt she might've seen before, and yet at the same time
she also felt she'd never seen. And there wasn't just one face. There
was another, and this one was familiar. Its lips parted to speak. "Stay.
Just stay here." As she and her family moved across the biting, wind-
blasted wilderness, she got the feeling that the voice echoed after
them for an eternity.

Exactly where her father and mother were trying to go she didn't know. At times, her mother looked back over her shoulder anxiously. While she realized they'd see nothing but desolate plains out there, her mother seemed to be afraid of something gaining on them. What made the girl uneasy was the unfamiliar face that hung in the heavens. Its eyes focused not on her father or mother but on herself—this the girl knew with every fiber of her being. The wind and bits of sand noisily struck the girl's face.

†

D was in the park. Sitting on a bench, he watched the water leaping in the fountain before him. As always, his thoughts were a mystery. A black shadow suddenly fell across his profile.

"Hey, are you D . . . ?" someone asked in a deep voice.

D didn't answer. It was almost as if he'd expected the question. The man standing by the end of the bench was a giant who seemed to stretch to the clouds. Not six or seven feet tall, but closer to ten. With a frame like a massive boulder with logs sunk in it for limbs, his shadow easily covered D and stretched to the base of the fountain several yards away. On the chest of his blue shirt there was a tiny, sharp gleam of light.

Apparently not taking very kindly to being ignored, the giant continued, "I'm Sheriff Hutton. Keeping the folks here in town safe from unsavory outsiders is what I do. And it don't matter whether you're the mayor's guest or not, that won't get you no slack from me. You wanna stay in town, you'd best mark your time peaceably and not go looking to stir up any trouble. See, if you put in three days on the job and have nothing to show for it, even the mayor will give up. I'm gonna be the one who goes looking for *your stinking kin*. I'll find 'im and drive a stake through his heart all proper-like. Being sheriff, I don't much cotton to them ignoring me and calling in a punk kid like you."

Hutton had a deadly piece of hardware by his right side—a rocket launcher that seemed to consist of seven barrels banded together. A piece of heavy machinery like that could blow away a large beast or even a small building with one shot. And stuck through his belt was a huge broadsword. Even without seeing his weapons, the average person needed only a glance at the size of their owner to start quaking in their boots. With just one look at the sheriff, some folks might even confess to crimes they hadn't even committed.

"I wanna know if you'll promise me something," the sheriff said. "Just tell me you'll leave town without doing anything. Don't worry—I'll tell the mayor you did your darnedest to take care of business. You follow me?"

There was no answer. The only thing about D that stirred was his hair, brushed by the wind. Vermilion started to tinge Sheriff Hutton's face. Slowly, he backed away. The business end of the rocket launcher he still had tucked under his arm jerked up. All seven barrels glared blackly at D.

"Don't think I'll give you any warning." The slight metallic click was the sound of the safety being disengaged. "I only give you the hint once. Ignoring it is the same as crossing me. And it wouldn't do the town a bit of good to let a fool like that go on living," the sheriff said, his voice cheery and his face bright.

An icy tone mixed with the wind. "You were one of the people who investigated the Knight house, weren't you? What was in there?"

"What the hell are you yammering about?!" the sheriff said, his voice taut, but he didn't do anything. He didn't even move the finger he had wrapped around the rocket launcher's trigger.

"Answer me," the voice said again. The Hunter's eyes were still trained on the white pillar of water spraying upward, making it difficult to say just who was grilling whom in this bizarre scene. Neither of the two moved, but in the space between them an invisible but nonetheless fierce battle was unfolding.

Strength surged into the sheriff's trigger finger. His weapon had been set to discharge all seven projectiles at once. In a matter of seconds, the bench and the young man sitting on it would be reduced to ash by a thirty-thousand-degree conflagration.

The faint sound of a siren pulled the weapon's muzzle from its target. Looking unexpectedly relieved, the sheriff's long face turned upward. Something more than just clouds resided in the azure sky. "Looks like the bastards have come for us. Damn, you're lucky. The next time I catch you alone, you'll wish to hell you'd left town when you had the chance."

The sheriff kept his eyes on the sky as he walked off, but D didn't give the lawman so much as a glance. When the Hunter finally did raise his face, the flapping shapes coming down from above could clearly be made out as birds. A siren stuttered to life like a suffocating person gasping for air. People bolted into the residential sector, stumbling along in their haste. D stood up.

A flock of predatory birds was on the attack. Ordinarily, these vicious monsters flew at altitudes of six thousand feet or more, and fed on the air beasts and flying jellyfish that lived at that height, but, when food became scarce, they'd come closer to earth. The larger ones had wingspans of over sixty feet. They could even carry off a giant cyclops. But the most frightening thing about them was that they didn't act alone, but rather always attacked in flocks of dozens. To their starving eyes, the moving town must've looked like one tremendous meal for the taking.

In the distance, the chatter of what sounded like machine-gun fire started. Streaks of flame rose to meet the approaching shapes. A black curtain swiftly fell over the streets. Around D, the stand of trees bent backward from the intense pressure of the wind.

Giving a stomach-churning caw, a bird with a wingspan of over fifteen feet swooped down like it was going to land right on top of D. Resembling a short horn, its beak was filled with nail-like teeth. Between wings beating incessantly with gale-force

winds, clawed feet were visible. Three digits as thick as tree roots went for D, hoping to catch him in their iron grip.

Silvery light flashed out. Though the Hunter's blade only seemed to paint a single arc, the colossal bird's wings were both cut down the middle, and fresh blood gushed from the creature's throat. The water spouting from the fountain was instantly dyed red. As D leapt away from the massive beast's falling corpse, other talons reached for him. Leaving only the crunch of severed bone in his wake, he slashed a gigantic leg off at the root.

A shrill scream filled the air. D turned around. Under a slowly rising pair of wings some fifteen feet away he saw a desperately struggling figure. It was a little girl in a long skirt. D ran directly under her and her captor. His left hand went into action. Leaving a white trail in its wake, the needle he hurled pierced the colossal bird at the base of its throat. Giving a shriek, the creature stopped flapping its wings and began losing altitude at an alarming rate.

A second later, D's expression changed. In an instant everything around him was black, as a hitherto unseen bird of prey with an enormous sixty-five-foot wingspan swooped down on the bird that had the girl, sank its claws into the base of the other bird's back, and started to rise again. The monstrous bird flapped its wings, and a tremendous shock wave hit the ground. Trees snapped, and the fountain's geyser blew horizontally. One after another, the window-panes of every house around the park shattered.

The hem of D's coat shielded his face. Was that all it took to negate the gale-force winds coming off the monstrous bird? Though the winds buffeted him, D's posture didn't change in the least as he stood his ground. When the avian monstrosity lifted its wings a second time, D kicked off the ground with incredible force. Flying almost straight up, he rose over fifteen feet. His extended left hand latched onto the ankle of the massive bird the other was carrying. Having taken a deadly blow to a vital spot, the lower bird was already dead. And the girl it had captured had fainted. Using his left hand as a fulcrum, D swung his body like a pendulum. In midair his coat opened and, adjusting for wind resistance, D sailed skillfully onto the back of the larger bird. The avian monstrosity roared. The harsh cry was not that of a bird, but of a vicious carnivore.

Holding his sword-point down, D raised the weapon high above his head. All at once, the wings of the monstrous bird swept back. Quivering, they gave off intense vibrational waves. The bird-like monstrosity's back became semitransparent. The agony of having a needle driven through each and every cell in his body assailed the Hunter. D's brow knit ever so slightly. That was his only reaction. The longsword he swiftly brought down pierced the monstrous bird right through the medulla oblongata.

A howl of pain shook the sky, and, when it ended, the breakup began. The creature's death throes must've turned the vibrations against its own anatomy, because every last feather came out of its wings, and its skin and flesh cracked like drying clay. In the blink of an eye, the monstrous bird of prey was reduced to numerous chunks of meat spread across the sky.

All this took place at an altitude of six hundred and fifty feet. Together, D and the little girl fell from the sky.

†

All told, it took the town two hours to fight off the birds of prey. Afterward, traces of the battle remained. Bright blood ran down the streets, several buildings had their roofs blown away by the wind pressure, and a boy who'd picked up a still-hot antiaircraft shell cried out in pain. The faces of the people were unexpectedly bright. There had been no fatalities. Hardly anyone had been wounded, either. A few people had received minor cuts from glass blown out of the windows, but that was the extent of the injuries. What's more, the food situation in town had started to show signs of improvement.

The smaller birds of prey were being loaded onto carts and hauled away, while men with axes and chainsaws gathered around the gigantic carcasses that filled the streets. The whine of motors mixed with sounds of meat and bones being severed, and here and there the stench of blood pervaded the town. In less than thirty minutes a huge bird with a thirty-foot wingspan could be stripped down to the point it was no longer recognizable. After all, man-eating birds were delicious, even to the very people they'd intended to eat.

The town was bustling with activity. Carts were laden with piles of meat, viscera, feathers, and bones to be hauled away. All of them would be sent to the factories for chemical processing, with some of the meat being preserved and sent to warehouses for storage. The rest would circulate to the butcher shops and turn up on dinner tables this very night. In the factories waited men with various skills at their disposal. Spears could be made from some of the bones, tendons and viscera could be used for bowstrings, and the rest of the skeleton would be pulverized to make a paste to be delivered to the hospital. Even the sharp fangs could be turned into accessories. And the blood had its uses as well—trace amounts of it would probably be mixed in juice or in their nightly drinks at the bar. The blood of birds of prey had been proven to have an invigorating effect on humans.

Among all of the bustling activity, a mother suddenly noticed her daughter was missing. Seeing her dashing all over town like a woman possessed as she called out the girl's name, other folks finally realized they hadn't seen the woman's only child anywhere. As someone tried to soothe the half-crazed mother, one of her friends answered that her daughter had been seen headed for the park. There was every reason to suspect the girl might've met her end at the talons of the colossal birds.

Several people started to dash down the street, but quickly stopped in their tracks. From the opposite direction came a beautiful yet foreboding young man. By his side was a slight figure. The woman called out the little girl's name and ran to her. As the mother and child shared a tearful embrace, D turned and walked away without giving them so much as a glance. Where was he going?

After the mother had brushed the little girl's hair away from her neck and confirmed there wasn't a mark on her, a relieved smile swept over her face.

"Didn't do nothing funny to you, now, did he?" said one man. "He's a dhampir, you know." Everyone muttered their shared sentiments at that.

"He saved me," the little girl mumbled.

"Saved you? From what?"

"A bird got me . . . Carried me way up into the sky . . . "

"You're talking nonsense. Nothing like that fell in the park."

"But it's true," the little girl said absentmindedly. "We were falling from the sky. And then he saved me . . . He really did save me."

The eyes of the townsfolk sought the young Hunter. But they could no longer find the faintest trace of him on the noisy street.

The Townsfolk

CHAPTER 3

I

Night fell and the clouds appeared, swirling shapes borne by the wind. The light of the moon was snuffed out.

This day—or to be more precise, this evening—was entirely without precedent for the town. Ordinarily, the streets would've been filled with merrymakers. Unwinding after a hard day's work, men with flushed faces would be arguing in bars where the lights burned all night and the hum of the electric organ never faded. Women would be harping about their daily toils while children dashed through the streets with newly acquired fireworks in hand. But tonight, shutters were lowered before the bar doors, and the wind alone danced through the streets. From time to time someone passed by, but they were volunteer deputies with deathly grim faces. The windows of every home were shut tight, and men ranged with weapons and sharpened stakes. For what was probably the first time ever, this town had to deal with the sort of rampaging demon all too familiar to those in the world below.

†

As soon as Laura had fallen asleep, the mayor called for D. "Now it's up to you." And saying only this, he left.

Putting the armchair they'd provided him against the wall, D sat down to wait. It was eleven o'clock Night. One of the most common times for the Nobility to pay a call. The young lady in bed breathed easily as she slept. But, though her breathing sounded serene enough, D heard another sound over it. Her breaths were just a bit longer and deeper than those of ordinary people. When she exhaled, her breathing sounded more like a sigh.

If the Noble who'd attacked the girl lived only by night, then the chances were extremely good that he wasn't aware D was here. No matter who was guarding the young lady, they'd certainly be no match for the power of a Noble. That was exactly the sort of self-confidence that led to mistakes. And all Vampire Hunters found that sense of security the key to destroying the Nobility.

An hour passed, and then two, without anything out of the ordinary. Both D and the girl seemed like statues, motionless. D had his eyes open.

At one o'clock Morning, there was a rapping sound outside the window. Laura's eyes snapped open. An evil grin of delight rose on her lips, and red light shone from her freshly opened eyes. As if checking just how they'd left her, she looked up above her, then to either side. When her eyes found D, they stopped dead. *Damned interloper*, they seemed to say.

Those who'd known the rapture in their blood didn't flee from it—rather, they were doomed to drown in it. Regardless of what she made of the Vampire Hunter sitting there with his eyes closed, after watching him for a while Laura turned her gaze beyond the window. "Who's there?" she asked coyly. She put the question to the pitch-black space.

Faint laughter came from the darkness. A voice that only the closest of human ears would hear said, "I'm coming in."

"You can't," she whispered back. "There's a Hunter in here."

"I don't have to fear the likes of him. Not even your father can touch me now."

"But he's not like other people," Laura said softly. "There's something different about him."

"Don't be ridiculous."

Something that looked like a black stain started flowing in through the window while the girl watched. Before Laura's very eyes it gathered on the floor, took human shape, and became an actual person of flesh and blood. This vampire was gifted with one of the powers of legend—that of entering rooms as a fog. The sight of him there, in an orange T-shirt and wrinkled jeans, would've made the bulk of the Nobility grimace. Still young, he was a powerfully built man. Yet his whole body was subtly distorted, looking like a human figure molded by the hands of a child . . .

Looking first at Laura, the vampire shifted his gaze to D. Sleeping, perhaps, D kept his face down and didn't move at all. The vampire's eyes began to glitter wildly. Red light tinged D's form a crimson hue. Soon, the light faded again.

"That'll keep him asleep," the intruder said. "Just as it did with the others. He won't even remember me."

"Oh, please hurry. Come to me . . ." Laura writhed beneath the blankets. "I want your kiss. I—I need . . . "

"I know." The vampire's lips twisted into a grin. Though his teeth were dirty and crooked, his canines were particularly impressive. They slanted forward. When he slowly bent over the girl, whose eyes were shut in rapture, the air in the room grew unspeakably cold. And the chill emanated from one point in particular. The intruder looked over his shoulder in disbelief. "You dirty bastard," he growled. "You mean to tell me my gaze didn't work on you?"

D got to his feet without saying a word.

Just as he was about to launch himself at the Hunter, the intruder stiffened. His already pale face lost even more color. D's aura had just hit him. *If I move, I'm as good as dead*, he thought.

"Any more of your kind around? Before you answer that, you'd better tell me your name," D commanded him softly. Calm as his voice was, it had a ring of steel to it that said no resistance would be tolerated. "Answer me. What's your name? Are you the only one?"

"No, I'm not . . . " the intruder replied.

"How many others are there?"

"One."

"What's your name, and what's theirs?"

The intruder began to tremble. Every inch of him shook, as if he were struggling against the threat that ensnared him.

"You don't have to tell me," D said. "If I check you against the resident lists, I should find out who you are. Step outside."

The man nodded. Slowly he made his way to the door to the front hall. D followed behind him. Something caught lightly at the Hunter's coat. Laura's pale hand. Most likely the action was merely a reflex, and not some effort to save the intruder. However, D's attention was diverted for a split second, and the spell he had over the other man broke. The intruder's body lost its shape. Wasting no time, the fog rushed for the door's keyhole like a black cloud and poured through it in a single stream.

D's right hand went into action. A flash as bright as the moon arced over his right shoulder, and the intruder who was supposedly safely on the other side of the door gave a scream of agonizing death. D's expression actually changed. Quickly opening the door, he peered beyond it—into the mayor's living room.

Before him was the intruder, now leaning backward. A sharp wooden tip poked from the left side of his back. From the waist down, the man remained in his fog-like condition. With a deep groan, the intruder fell to the floor, both hands clutching his own throat. It seemed that the fog was probably his true form after all. His fallen body soon covered itself in a black hue and curled up on the floor with a rustling sound.

"What do you think you're doing?" D's quiet tone harbored an unearthly air.

"Nothing, I was just . . . " Dr. Tsurugi stammered, shaking his head. "I heard a strange sound and I froze in my tracks, trying to figure out what I should do, when all of a sudden . . . My eyes met his, and then I just panicked and ran him through."

Not saying a word, D merely gazed at bits of fog spreading across the floor and the stake dripping with black blood. "How did you get in here?" the Hunter finally asked. His voice was far more terrifying than any heated tone could've been.

"I snuck in," said Dr. Tsurugi, giving the sack over his shoulder a pat. There was a loud clatter that suggested it contained a hammer and stakes. "But everything's taken care of now, right?"

"It seems we face two foes." Heedless of the changes those words wrought on the physician's expression, the Hunter continued. "One may be gone now, but we don't know the whereabouts of the other. Are you sure there haven't been any other victims? None at all?"

Dr. Tsurugi nodded.

"The girl's probably back to normal," said D. "Go check on her."

"Sure," the young physician replied, and he was just about to nod his head. Then his eyes halted at the legs of the corpse that'd been reduced to dust. There was a gap of a fraction of an inch just below the knees. "It almost looks like . . . You cut him, didn't you?"

Giving no reply, D squatted down by the dusty remains. Once he was sure Dr. Tsurugi had gone through the door, the Hunter stretched his left hand over the dust. "How about it?" he asked.

"Oh, this is a tough one," a hoarse voice said in reply. "The memory's been completely erased from the cells. But then, I guess you already know this guy wasn't made to serve any Noble." Was the voice suggesting, then, that this vampire had just spontaneously generated?

Not surprised in the least, D nodded. "But those who aren't Nobility don't just turn into Nobles on their own."

"Then that'd mean someone had to make him that way," the voice suggested. "What we've got here is an imitation vampire. The question is, who made it?"

D didn't reply.

"Come to think of it, they did say something about letting someone into town two centuries ago. Could be him again . . . " the hoarse voice mused. "Still, it's all very strange. From what the mayor's said, and from the way the locals have been acting, it doesn't seem like there's been a ruckus over vampires before. So, these characters suddenly show up two hundred years after the fact? There's no way their strange visitor could still be in town after all this time. What do you think?"

Straightening up, D headed for the mayor's room. "There's another one out there," he said. "That's all I know."

When the Hunter knocked on his door, the mayor stuck his head out like he'd been waiting for him to come. "What is it?" he asked.

"He's been taken care of."

"My daughter's been saved?"

"Ask the doctor about that."

Just as the mayor's dazed face turned toward his daughter's bedroom, Dr. Tsurugi appeared. Seeing the mayor, he gave a satisfied smile. The mayor's shoulders dropped and a deep sigh escaped from him. "Can I see her?"

Not saying a word, D stepped aside. The mayor disappeared into his daughter's bedroom.

"Remarkable, isn't it?" As D was headed for the front door, the odd remark followed him. It was neither praising nor sarcastic, but the tone of it was nearly a challenge. "This thing had everyone quaking in their boots, but you come here and things get taken care of in no time flat . . . Although it was yours truly that put the fateful stake through his heart."

"Yes, it was." D turned around.

A strangely firm resolve, or something like it, graced the young physician's face. It was an unusual emotion, one no one had ever directed toward D.

The mayor quickly came back out of his daughter's room. A smile spread across his face, and he declared, "The wounds on her throat have vanished, and she's sleeping peacefully. And all thanks to you, D!"

"If you'll pardon me saying so, I was actually the one who finished him off."

Looking dumbfounded, the mayor turned from D to Dr. Tsurugi and back again.

"The doctor's right," D told him. "I was no use at all."

"Don't be ridiculous," Dr. Tsurugi countered vehemently. "Mayor, this gentleman not only prevented the sneaking vampire from laying a finger on your daughter, but also succeeded in driving him from her room. I merely happened to be in the right place at the right time. If any reward is to be paid, we'll split it."

"You're welcome to it," D said, sounding somewhat surprised. His tone was strangely agreeable. Perhaps he was taken aback by events.

"I'd like you to come to my room," the mayor said with a smile. "You'll be given your remuneration. We'll put you up wherever you like in town. Why, if you should decide to stay on permanently with us, that'd be fine, too."

"Can't do that just yet." In the present mood of jubilant confidence, the Hunter's words hung like icicles. "There's still another one out there."

"What?" the mayor began to say, but his mouth merely hung open. "Impossible!"

"No. He said there were two of them. I don't think he was lying."

"But—" the mayor sputtered, "You see, up till now there haven't been any victims aside from my Laura."

D turned to the physician. Gathering the drift of his question from that look alone, the physician shook his head. "No one's come to my hospital secretly for treatment."

"When was the town's last regular medical exam?"

"A week ago. There were some colds and minor chronic conditions, but there wasn't anyone out of the ordinary. No one skipped the medical exams. I can guarantee that."

"The last time his daughter was attacked was three days ago. How about since then?"

"I can't vouch for anyone after that."

Letting out a deep sigh, the mayor brought his fist to his forehead. "A fine mess we have here. One problem solved, and another arises to take its place. Now we hear our town—a town our foes in the outside world can't even get into—has been invaded by not one but *two* filthy freaks."

"Only two if we're lucky," Dr. Tsurugi said, his expression greatly changed. "You just happened to find out about your daughter, but there may well be other victims who've been bitten without anyone noticing. They might not yet have turned into vampires. In some cases, their families may keep them hidden, too."

"Exactly," D said with a nod.

While humans feared the Nobility to their very marrow, the love they felt for their own flesh and blood sometimes prevailed over their terror when a member of their family became one of the undead. Many were the families who'd watch their child growing thinner and paler each night and think it better to hide them in some back room of the house rather than have them run out of the village. That was usually the case when a whole family became dark disciples of the vampires. Love thinks little of courting death. When the fangs of the very child they'd risked their life to defend coldly pressed against their carotid artery, was it a feeling of remorse that skimmed through the mother or father's heart? Or was it satisfaction?

"I suppose it would be best if we didn't inform anyone that one vampire's been destroyed?" said the mayor.

Both D and Dr. Tsurugi nodded.

"This may sound a bit odd," the physician began, "but you'll have to keep Laura from leaving the house. We want folks in town to believe this incident hasn't been resolved— because, in fact, it hasn't. Mr. D and I can handle the search."

D donned an unusual expression. The man in the white lab coat seemed intent on running the show. The problem was, he really didn't look like the pushy type. It was almost as if D's presence brought it out in him.

"Actually," the mayor began, craning his neck uncomfortably, "that's a job for the law enforcement bureau. I'll have to let them know about this."

"As they haven't been able to accomplish anything to date," D replied, "I don't imagine they'll be of much more use in the future. Leave everything to me. And talk some sense into the good doctor, too."

"Understood. Dr. Tsurugi, I'd like you to remain silent regarding this incident, and keep out of the investigation. Those are my orders as mayor."

"But—" Dr. Tsurugi began indignantly before restraining himself. "Very well, sir. As disappointing as it may be, I'll refrain from joining Mr. D in his work. And now, if you'll excuse me." Bidding them adieu in a loud voice, the young physician squared his sturdy shoulders and disappeared into the darkness outside.

"Another one?" the mayor mumbled, sounding very weary.

"Another one—and we have to wait until he claims another victim," D muttered. "The doctor must've seen the vampire's face. He didn't say anything in particular about it, though."

"You mean as to whether or not it was someone from town?"

Ignoring the question, D said, "When's the last time you had a death or a missing person?"

Squinting, the mayor replied, "Last death would be two years ago, missing person would go three or four months back. Exact cause isn't known, but most likely they got drunk and fell off the town. I'll make you a list of names and addresses."

D nodded.

†

II

The next morning, there was a rap at the door of D's assigned lodgings that created quite a racket.

"It's open," a low voice responded, but whoever knocked made no attempt to open to the door. "What is it?" the Hunter asked.

"Um, it's the mayor and Dr. Tsurugi. They want you to come right away. Someone's sick. Come to the A Block of the industrial sector." After these fear-filled words, there was the sound of furtive footsteps fading away.

Rising from his simple bed of hay without a word, D made his necessary preparations. Of course, those preparations consisted simply of strapping his longsword to his back.

†

The sun was already high. People on the street watched in terror as D walked by, his stride smooth as the wind. The industrial sector was on the edge of town. It consisted of three colossal blocks of buildings in a row. Aside from the actual energy used to keep the town in flight, everything they needed for their day-to-day existence was produced in the industrial blocks. It was the town's lifeline, so to speak.

Without needing to see the A Block markings on the doors, D was guided there by the otherworldly atmosphere. A few people were standing at the entrance to a semi-cylindrical dome. The mayor and doctor were among them. And, of course, the sheriff, with the silver rocket-launcher tucked under his arm. Some men, perhaps deputies, were pushing back a wall of people to keep them from getting any closer. As D approached, the mass of humanity parted smoothly, making a path for him. Gazes brimming with fatigue, astonishment, and hatred greeted the Hunter.

At the mayor's feet lay a man. A white waterproof sheet shrouded him. Keeping his silence, D went down on one knee and lifted the sheet. Under it was a middle-aged man, around forty years old. Eyes thrown wide open and lips zipped tight, his features were a detailed testament to a moment so horrifying he couldn't even scream.

"What's the story?" D asked quietly.

"Like you need me to tell you," the sheriff replied snidely. "There ain't a damn drop of blood left in his body. One of your pals must've sucked him dry."

"That doesn't seem to be what happened," D said, turning to Dr. Tsurugi.

The physician nodded. "Indeed, all the blood's missing from this body. However, there are no signs of a bite."

"Check 'im good enough and you'll find a bite, all right," said the sheriff. "At any rate, we've got another victim now. If you keep relying on some clown we don't know from a hole in the ground, we're gonna have a few more on our hands, too. Mayor, I think it's high time you let my office handle this. You leave it to us. Inside of seventy-two hours we'll smoke that freak out and get rid of anyone who's been bitten."

Mayor Ming's face was warped with anguish.

"Though the symptoms are the same," D said, "this isn't the work of the Nobility, or even of one of their victims. You won't find a mark on him. My guess is . . . "

Dr. Tsurugi was already nodding in agreement. "This could very well be some new kind of illness."

"What?! Now I know you two bastards have gotta be in cahoots!" the sheriff bellowed.

"I'd like another three days," said D. "If I haven't found your foe by then, I'll leave town."

"You've gotta be out of your fucking—"

"Good enough," said the mayor, cutting off the sheriff. "For the next three days, the search for the vampire is entirely in the hands of Mr. D. Sheriff, you're not to interfere with him in any way at all."

Though his whole face flushed vermilion, the sheriff held his tongue.

"A wise course of action," Dr. Tsurugi said, his back to the gigantic lawman.

"You little bastard . . . " the sheriff growled, latching onto the physician's shoulder with his meaty fingers. And then something wrapped around the lawman's wrist. The mayor's arm.

"Sheriff," the mayor said to the face of naked ferocity that greeted him. Just one word. The vermilion hue of excitement faded from the sheriff's face in a matter of seconds.

"Okay. You're the mayor. What you say, goes. But he only gets three days. And during that time, he ain't gonna get a bit of help from us. He'll have to do all the questioning and all the investigating all by his lonesome. And I'll tell you one thing—this here town's pretty damn big." And then he left, with his men following close behind.

"Well, then, about this body . . ." Dr. Tsurugi said, rubbing his eyelid. "Should we bring it to the morgue, or back to the hospital? Personally, I'd love a chance to dissect it. He didn't have any family, correct?"

The mayor nodded.

"Then we'll bring it back to the hospital for the time being. We can't discount the possibility this is some sort of illness."

On orders from the mayor, two of the townsfolk were selected and, one at each end of a stretcher, they loaded the body onto the back of the hospital motorcycle parked nearby.

"Well, then, I'll be running on ahead."

The young physician departed, leaving only the growl of an engine in his wake. That left only D and the mayor. A forceful wind gusted around the two of them. Perhaps it was a gale that blew from the light into darkness. Or maybe it was something else.

"What is it?" the mayor said succinctly. "You think it could be an illness?"

D didn't answer him. This was probably the first time he'd found a corpse that'd been drained of blood but didn't have a mark on it. "I don't know for sure. We need Dr. Tsurugi to hurry with that analysis. Depending on how this plays out, it may become necessary for him to come up with a vaccine. If that's the case, he will need to do it quickly."

"Then you do think it's a disease after all . . . " Beads of greasy sweat blossomed across the mayor's brow.

†

Sitting in a block of sunlight spearing through her window, the girl pondered the fate that lay ahead of her. She couldn't speak or hear. Dr. Tsurugi had given her the truth quite plainly. And she felt like she'd plunged straight into hell. She would be forced to live in a world stripped of all sound, where she couldn't convey a single thought unless she had a pen in her hand. The physician had tried to console her by saying that she wouldn't be left with any scars from the radiation poisoning, but what would that matter?

How old am I, again? The girl tried doing the math once more. *Seventeen.* At that age, her whole life was still ahead of her. And it'd all been wiped out. When she'd first found out what'd happened, she couldn't think of anything at all. She just wanted to die. And then *he* had come. The beautiful face of the man they said had saved her was lodged in her brain. Entirely too gorgeous and completely noncommittal. *He saved me,* the girl thought, obsessed with the notion. *Oh, I hope he comes to see me again. Just one more time.*

A number of sounds passed right by the girl. The footsteps of the physician and nurse as they went down the corridor. The creaking of the gurney bearing what looked to be a dead body. A voice filled with revulsion. Sounds from things like the generator and an electric saw passed right through the thin walls, stirring the girl's hair. Perhaps you could say she was lucky not to have to hear any of that.

So, what happens next? This thought alone continued to occupy the girl's mind. Before she knew it, the light outside her window had taken an azure tint. She had no idea whether the doctor and nurse were in the next room or not. Once the light was gone, she'd be separated from them by an eternal gulf.

Just then, she saw a figure reflected in the door across from her. As she watched, something like a black stain appeared in one part of the glass, soon spreading across its entirety like a flower opening its petals in a time-lapse film. Before the girl's very eyes, the stain quickly became a black mass of sorts, its contours shifting faintly as it approached her bed. The girl inched back in spite of herself. She was just about to press the emergency call button when a black hand deftly reached over and snatched it away.

Well, can you understand what I'm saying?

Piercing thoughts crept into her head. The girl's eyes went wide with astonishment.

Don't be so surprised. It's called telepathy. With it, a person can make their thoughts understood without ever speaking. Even a young lady with no voice. Would you care to try it?

The girl nodded. She moved her head so vigorously it almost looked like some sort of exercise.

Okay, I'll show you how to do it. But in return, there's something I want to ask you. Will you answer me?

The girl nodded. As her eyes gazed at the unsettling black mass, they seemed to cling to it for dear life.

I understand certain experiments were conducted at your house. The voice rang through her head, and it was accompanied by a delightful stimulation. *The secret of that research is hidden somewhere in your house. Tell me where. No, you don't need to say it. Think it.*

The girl shut her eyes. Gathering up all she remembered of the life they'd once lived, she began searching for some concrete example of the experiments her father had undertaken. Coming away empty-handed, the girl conveyed that result.

That can't be! The shadowy figure's thoughts were like flames. *Your father was involved in forbidden experiments. And only he was able to make them succeed. Answer me. You must remember!*

The question burned in the girl's brain like molten steel. Her whole body trembling, she collapsed on the bed. At that moment, the door opened. The shadowy figure seemed to look that way.

"What the hell are you?" Dr. Tsurugi shouted, his words spreading across the room like a wildfire.

The shadow turned to face the physician without making a sound. Perhaps it was his youth, or maybe he was just reckless, but the physician spread his arms wide and tried to grab hold of the shadowy figure. His hands sank into the intruder's form. Not just that—the shadow actually passed right through the physician's body. Molecular intangibility was at work.

"Hey," Dr. Tsurugi shouted as he raced to Lori's side, though he had no idea what was going on. "Are you okay?" he asked.

Managing to follow the movement of his lips, Lori nodded in reply.

Noticing the pale blue phosphorescence of his own limbs, the physician pulled back in surprise. That was the aftereffect of the molecular intangibility. "Looks like I'll have to take something for radiation, too," the physician said absentmindedly, smiling at Lori.

But in her mind, the shadow's thoughts still pulsed. *You can use telepathy, too*, the shadow had said.

†

The body of the deceased citizen was to be buried in the town's cemetery. According to the autopsy, death had resulted from massive and rapid loss of blood—that was all they could tell. The corpse had been checked from the top of its head to the tips of its toes, but, aside from a few minor abrasions, there wasn't any sign of the fateful wound. As they carried the coffin with the man's corpse to the cemetery, everyone thought the same thing.

When the sun goes down, he's gonna get up. After the undertaker's secondhand robots had finished digging the hole, the corpse was laid to rest. The soil was shoveled back in, and the undertaker— who doubled as a reverend—intoned several words of prayer. And with that, the man was firmly laid to rest with the past.

Soon after, the sun went down. Not a single person remained around this desolate patch of earth, but then a woman of about thirty came with a hurried gait. She was the wife of the man who ran the general store. But there was something strange about the way she walked. It looked like she was being called forward, and didn't care for it one bit. As the woman moved forward, she threw her head back, dug her heels in, and was tugged along.

Presently, she stood before the fresh grave. Brushing her cheek against the mounded dirt so it rustled against her skin, she then got to her feet again. Hunching over, with a frightened expression and a chilling grin, she began digging into the fresh grave. With every movement of her hands, a vast quantity of earth was thrown behind her. In no time she had made a small mountain of dirt. Even though the soil was loose from the recent burial, the sheer volume of it was extraordinary.

When the lid of the wooden box could be seen at the bottom of the hole, the woman's lips twisted in an expression of sheer delight. What a blackly evil smile it was. The hole was ten feet deep. The woman stared at the box. The sun had already sunk beyond the edge of the plains. Nothing but the white street lights threw any illumination on the woman's deeds.

Slowly the coffin began to rise. As if pushed up by the earth itself it ascended, not the least bit unsteady as it approached the lip of the hole. Anxiety and rapture intertwined in the woman's countenance.

Rising clean out of the grave, the coffin stopped level with the woman's chin. The lid of the box opened from the inside, pushed open by a pale hand. With the same gingerly pace at which the box had risen from the grave, the dead man sat up. Still seated in the coffin, he turned to the woman and smirked. Pearly canines jutted from his mouth. His eyes gave off a red glow. With a look from him, the woman was completely stripped of her freedom. She smiled back at him. With strangely stiff movements, the man climbed down to the ground. The coffin stayed right where it was.

The man came closer. Saying nothing, the woman waited. For the first time it dawned on her that in life this man had been in love with her. There was a short, soft whistle, and at that point something stuck in the nape of the man's neck. A thin needle of unfinished wood.

"Sorry to say this, but that's as far as you go," a low voice said. To the man's right there was a rustling of tree branches. The man was at a loss for words. "And since you've risen again, I take it you know what the person who did this to you looks like. Tell me."

Even if the man had wanted to answer, he was still pierced through the throat. Needle stuck in his neck, the man leapt back a good six feet, and at the same time the woman crumpled to the ground.

"You must be destroyed," D said coldly. "But before you go, you should leave the world of daylight something. How about it?"

The man reached for the end of the needle with his right hand. He had no difficulty pulling out the wooden shaft D had hurled at him. A stream of blood squirted from the wound. The man pursed his lips.

D raised his left hand. Holding it flat and straight like a knife, he moved forward. The red stream that issued from the man's mouth was split down the middle by the edge of the Hunter's hand, and both halves vanished in the darkness. But D sensed white smoke rising from the ground where the man's blood had fallen.

"Quite a strange power you have there," the Hunter remarked. "But now the end is at hand." Not giving the man a second chance to purse his lips, D covered him completely with his coat. The moment it opened again, the man fell to the ground unconscious as if jerked down by ropes. Looking down at the man, D said softly, "I've taken care of him. Come out now."

"Thanks a bunch." There was the sound of branches shaking in a thicket some fifteen or twenty feet away, and then a fairly limber figure appeared. "So, you've got a trick that can knock a Noble's underling out in one shot? When you've got a little time to kill, I'd love to see how you do that." Punctuating his last comment with a burst of cackling laughter was none other than John M. Brasselli Pluto VIII.

"Why are you out here?" D asked.

"Aw, don't get all tough with me, partner." Pluto VIII smiled at the Hunter, his expression intimating they'd been friends for ages. "I knew he was bound to come back to life, so I was just waiting around for it. I tell you, that was a hell of a fight you gave that critter. I'm impressed. Very impressed!"

"What are you after?" D asked softly.

"Not a thing," Pluto VIII replied, shaking his head in earnest. If he was tortured to the point where he could no longer speak, he could probably get by on that gesture alone.

"It doesn't matter. Just stay out of the way."

"Yes, sir." It was hard to tell just what was going through Pluto VIII's head, but for some reason he gave the Hunter a round of applause, then said, "By the way, were you by any chance planning on taking this creep back with you and making 'im spill his guts?"

"What are you talking about?"

"It's pretty obvious, ain't it? You aim to find out just who went and made this character like this. After all, he lost all that blood but doesn't have a scratch on him. How weird is that?! You've gotta look into what's causing this."

"You're exactly right." Easily carrying the fanged man on one shoulder and the unconscious woman on the other, D turned away.

"Hey, hold on! Wait just a minute," Pluto VIII cried out excitedly, scampering after the Hunter. "Let me carry the lady. I tell you, I can't believe how tough it is trying to crack the gals in this here town. I can talk myself blue in the face, but they won't give me the time of day. I should take this opportunity to make a reputation for myself."

While it wasn't quite clear whether the Hunter was dumbfounded or not, as D stood there Pluto VIII basically pried the woman away from him and cradled her body in his arms. "Buddy, do you seriously think this character is just gonna tell you everything? I mean, after all, he's a freaking vampire!"

D said nothing.

"I'll let you in on a little secret. I can get him to spill his guts for you. I'll let you ask him whatever you want, just let me get some questions in, too."

D stopped in his tracks. As he slowly turned, Pluto VIII must've sensed something in the Hunter's face, and, giving a cry of surprise, the biker leapt back a good ten feet. "Didn't I tell you not to look at me all serious like that? Just thinking about that mug of yours gives me a powerful urge to jerk off, you know. At this rate, I'm liable to fall in love with you if you don't watch it."

"Just what are you up to?"

"Not a blessed thing."

"Should I talk to the mayor and have him toss you out of town?"

"Won't do you a bit of good," Pluto VIII chortled. "I figured you might try something like that, so I found myself a new hideout. Besides, you can't even find where the vampire's holed up. You know, I wouldn't be a bit surprised if you wound up with another one on your hands." What Pluto VIII said was right on the mark. "So, what'll it be? Stop looking so grim and make up your mind already."

"Okay," D said softly with a nod.

†

Where Pluto VIII finally led D was to an abandoned boardinghouse next to C Block in the industrial sector. "What do you think? Pretty great, huh? Got myself three rooms here. Can cook up my grub wherever I please. You're looking at the lord of the manor," Pluto VIII said pompously. "It don't matter to me if you tell anyone else where to find me. Given five minutes, I can move myself into another hideout, you know. I'm a slipperier eel than any vampire."

"What are you really after?" asked D.

"Who do you think you're dealing with here?" Pluto VIII said, settling himself into a plastic chair. He invited D to do the same, but the Hunter wouldn't sit down. The woman from the general store had been left lying next to a street that saw a lot of pedestrian traffic in a place where someone was sure to find her right away. Anyone summoned by a vampire's power, as she had been, wouldn't remember a single thing that had happened while under the vampire's spell. Pluto VIII had set the unconscious vampire down on a large bed of rather simple tastes. Fingering the fiend's extended canine teeth with morbid curiosity, he said, "Well, now. Let's see if we can't get him to answer two or three questions. Okay, now watch closely."

Saying that, he clambered onto the bed and over to where he'd put the vampire, then laid down on his back right next to the other man. D saw him squeeze down on the vampire's hand. Pluto VIII closed his eyes. As he did so, all trace of expression vanished from his face. At the same time, the vampire began to tremble all over and his eyes opened wide.

"Pretty slick, eh?" the vampire said in Pluto VIII's voice. While the face was still clearly that of a farmhand, the expression had taken on an indefinable fullness, and through the eyes and mouth it bore a distinct likeness to Pluto VIII. This little stub of a man actually had the ability to possess other bodies. "Damn, it's cold," he groaned. "Inside this guy's head and all through his body it's just one great big winter wonderland. On the other hand, being in here I know everything he's thinking. Now, according to him, he got turned into a vampire by . . . wow, by no one at all. All of a sudden he got cold and fell to the ground in front of that factory. And that's about the size of it, it seems. Ain't that the damnedest thing!"

"Is the illness contagious?"

To D's question, Pluto VIII replied, "I don't know. What I can tell you is he's got a powerful thirst for blood. That's it." Suddenly Pluto VIII's voice became muddled. Malevolence flooded into his normally amiable expression. His face now that of a demon, he leapt to his feet. The human who'd possessed this vampire had been overthrown with remarkable ease. Imitation vampire or not, the mental powers that condition endowed the victim with were certainly formidable. Slowly, the demon headed toward D—and then he suddenly grinned from ear to ear, just like Pluto VIII. "Sorry about that," he laughed in the biker's voice. "Didn't mean to alarm you—not that you budged an inch. Well, I guess that's D for you. So, that's the only question you've got?"

"No, I have another. What in the world were they researching in that house?"

"Can't say," Pluto VIII replied indifferently. "He's probably got the information, but everything related to it is in a fog. Guess that means no answer."

Nothing from D.

"Looks like our plan has run awry."

D gave a slight nod.

One of the paranormal phenomena that often linked the bloodsucker to its prey was a transference of memories. Often the memories of a vampire were copied into the brain of his or her victim. In most cases what was transferred was only a small portion of vampire's recollections, but there were some victims who wound up with all of a Noble's memories. By sending his consciousness into the other man's body, Pluto VIII had hoped to access any memories that might've belonged to whoever made him.

Not saying a word, D slung the undead body over his shoulder.

"Hey, what're you doing?!" the corpse—or rather, Pluto VIII—shouted.

"If we're through with him, I have to get him back in his grave. If you want to get out of him, better be quick about it."

"What a selfish little ingrate you are," the man sneered, and then all stiffness left his body. At the same instant, Pluto VIII's body got up from where it'd been lying on the bed. "I'll have you know it takes a good deal of mental preparation to leap from one body to another. Oh, I think I'm gonna be sick—"

D left the biker's room without making a sound.

†

As it moved forward, the town seemed to be glaring down at the brown plains. A group of shepherds and merchants looked up at it enviously and waved. Offering them nothing in return, the town continued its remorseless advance. But one had to wonder if it was actually making any progress. The town went on diligently, headed straight for the sun as it shone down with a strangely spiteful hue.

†

The next day, D called on the twenty or so men listed on the mayor's sheet as being involved in boarding up the Knight family's home. All of them gave him the same reply. No one had seen or heard anything strange while they were moving things out of the house. The mysteries of that abode remained shrouded in fog. As D was getting ready to call on the last person on the list, Sheriff Hutton, someone behind him called out his name. It was Dr. Tsurugi. Turning around, D asked, "How did it go?"

"His condition remains unchanged. I wasn't able to learn anything from the corpse." He was referring to the man who'd risen from his grave the previous night. D had carried the body Pluto VIII had occupied to Dr. Tsurugi and had him subject it to a second medical examination. "It's certainly my opinion this was caused by some sort of viral infection, but at the moment I can't seem to put my finger on the culprit."

"There'll be trouble if you can't." That was all D said.

Realizing just what kind of trouble the Hunter was talking about, Dr. Tsurugi used the back of his hand to wipe away the sweat he'd just realized was pouring from him. Cold sweat.

"I'll see you later," D said, turning his back.

"Wait a minute," the physician called out to him.

"What is it?"

The young physician shyly scratched at his head, which seemed to be a habit with him. "If you don't mind, do you think you could pay a visit with me? To Lori Knight, I mean. She's been acting a bit strangely."

"Strangely?"

"Yes. Ever since she was attacked by this weird, shadowy character yesterday, her behavior's been rather unusual."

"My going to see her wouldn't change anything."

"Well, by not going you certainly won't do her any good."

"Then you'll have to wait until I've taken care of one bit of business," D said, and began to walk away. Twisting and turning through a number of streets and back alleys, he arrived at the law enforcement bureau. Pushing his way through a cracked glass door patched together with strips of heavy tape, he made his way inside.

Sitting behind his desk with his feet up while he joked with a couple of his deputies, the giant developed a sudden twitch in his face as soon as he caught sight of D. "What brings you here?" he asked. "You still got two days left. Don't tell me you want off already?"

"I have business with you," D said plainly. "Could I speak to you in private?"

Struck perhaps by the Hunter's chilling aura, the two deputies quickly got to their feet, but the sheriff pushed them back down with hands the size of catcher's mitts. "Wait just a cotton-picking minute, boys. This here's the law enforcement bureau. We don't take orders from no outsider. Least of all from a stinking Vampire Hunter. You're not going anywhere. You'll sit right here with me and hear what he's got to say, you savvy? So, how's that by you?" The last remark was aimed at D.

D nodded. "Doesn't matter to me. I just have one question for you. When you were boarding up the Knight house, did you see anything?"

"What do you mean by 'anything'?" The sheriff laughed, showing a lot of yellow teeth.

"Were there any unusual items? Strange drugs, papers with formulas or equations? Special creatures? Anything like that."

The sheriff snorted loudly, "Of course there wasn't a damn thing like that."

"Then I have another question for you. Why did the Knight family leave town?"

"You might wanna ask the mayor that."

"Did the whole town drive them away, or—"

"Or what?"

"Or were they glad to leave? Which was it?"

"You come here looking to start trouble, buster?!" Sheriff Hutton snarled. The two deputies braced themselves for action. The sheriff started to rise from his oversized chair. His rear was only about an inch out of the chair when he stopped dead in his tracks. D was standing right in front of him. He was just standing there, an unearthly aura radiating from every inch of his body. That alone kept not only the sheriff but his two deputies as well from moving a muscle.

"Answer me straight," said D.

"You—you gotta be fuckin' kidding me," the sheriff blustered, but his voice quivered nevertheless.

"In that case, you leave me no choice."

Raising his left hand, D pressed it against the sheriff's forehead. The same vacuous expression seen on a mental defective spread across the sheriff's face. Eyes covered with a semitransparent film and drool coursing from the corner of his mouth, the lawman stared vacantly into space.

"Why did the family leave town?"

A reply wasn't soon in coming. No doubt a battle was raging in the sheriff's mind, a battle between his own ego and D's words. The only question was how it all would end.

"That family . . . was doing freaky experiments . . . Don't know all the particulars . . ." The words were clearly being torn from the sheriff. And it went without saying the power of D's left hand was to blame.

"You knew that, and still you did nothing?" the Hunter asked.

"Wanted to . . . but then . . . mayor stopped me."

"The mayor?" D's eyes shone. "Why would he do that?"

"Don't know . . . But I had official orders . . . Wasn't supposed to do anything . . . about that family . . . ever . . . Seems the sheriff before me . . . had the same orders."

"How long had it been going on?"

"From way back . . . Roughly two hundred years . . ."

According to what the mayor had said, that was right around the time the eerie stranger had come on board.

"And their strange experiments had been going on all that time?"

"I . . . I wouldn't know . . ."

"Was the Knight family run out of town, or did they leave of their own accord?"

"They . . . ran away . . ."

"Ran away?"

"Night before they run off . . . mayor gave me orders . . . I went to their house . . . Knights were there . . . Arrested 'em on the spot . . . just like the mayor told me to . . . Threw 'em . . . in jail . . . Daughter was with them, of course . . . Mayor never did tell me . . . why we had to do that . . . Just said they'd committed a serious offense . . . against the whole town . . . and that was all."

"I see."

The "offense," then, was experiments the Knight family had been conducting for generations. But what reason would the mayor—

who'd always supported the Knights—have for ordering their arrest? And what could they have told the mayor?

"How did Mr. and Mrs. Knight seem?"

"I don't know . . . They weren't scared . . . at all . . . The two of them . . . looked to be giving some serious thought to something . . . What it was . . . I don't know."

"How did they get away?"

"The next day . . . I go for a look . . . and the cell wall . . . was melted away. Mr. Knight was a chemist . . . Figure he had something hidden on him . . . Acid or something . . . "

"I'll be seeing you again." D's hand came away from the sheriff.

It wasn't until the hem of the Hunter's black coat was well out the door that the sheriff and his two men collapsed into their chairs as if utterly exhausted.

†

Dr. Tsurugi was waiting for D. "I realize you must be busy, but I'd really like for you to come with me," he said.

D nodded. "I said I would. Let's go."

The two of them set off for the hospital.

"Quiet town," said D.

"I guess it is, at that. The sheriff and mayor probably have a pretty easy time keeping the peace. They don't get strangers coming in and causing trouble. And the townsfolk are all well-behaved types who follow the rules. Every so often someone gets a little rough, but no one's any rougher than the sheriff."

A smile formed on D's lips. "Except for you," he said.

Dr. Tsurugi didn't say anything, but he gave a great big grin. Quickly looking to D again, he asked, "How long will you be in town?"

"If I was done, I could leave tomorrow." And then, in a rare move for the Hunter, he asked in return, "How about you?"

"Well, my contract is for a full year. But I suppose I'll be getting off before then."

"Wouldn't it cause problems if their doctor were to leave town?"

"Nothing they couldn't solve by finding another physician," Dr. Tsurugi replied.

"Are you bored?"

"Don't be ridiculous. You wouldn't think it to look at me, but I studied a bit of psychology. And from a psychological standpoint, you couldn't find a more intriguing place. By their very nature, towns on the Frontier must exercise rather rigid controls in order to protect themselves from enemies without, but here they've taken it to the furthest extreme. Where do you think this town is headed?"

D gave no reply.

"Actually, they wander the earth far and wide with no goal at all."

"People down on the ground don't have a goal, either. Humans, Nobility—all of creation is that way," D said.

"Yes, but in a village, people come in. In towns, people leave. Here, there's neither. Do you have any idea how much time and energy the people of this town invest to come up with drugs that combat the problems caused by inbreeding? In my humble opinion, the only folks in town in their right mind were the Knights."

"Do you know anything about them?" the Hunter asked.

"Unfortunately, no."

"I suppose this place might not suit you. You like traveling then, do you?"

The young physician nodded. It was a deep, hearty nod. His dark eyes sparkled. "Yes. I've met all kinds of people. You might say I became a doctor because I like to travel. The Frontier's not completely hopeless. No matter what they've been dealt there, everybody's giving life all they've got. I bet the same is true for the remaining Nobility. And I just want to help folks do that."

Saying nothing, D continued walking. But in his eyes was something that looked incredibly like a bit of warmth. The young physician failed to notice how his words had brought about a minor miracle.

"You're a dhampir, correct? Been traveling long?"

"A bit longer than you," D replied

"I'll be like you before too long," the physician said in a fervent tone. "I suppose I'll get as experienced as you are. Along the way, I'll learn how to ride and how to use a sword."

Though the young doctor's words sounded almost like a challenge, D remained silent.

Presently, the pair arrived at the hospital. The nurse walked just ahead of them, escorting them to the sickroom. Over the course of the ten feet or so they had to go, the nurse nearly crashed into a table, almost put her hand through a window pane, and had to be caught by the physician after tripping over the threshold . . . All because she could do nothing but look at D.

Some pink discoloration remained on Lori's skin. That was the extent of her injuries. Apparently the plasters for drawing the radioisotopes from her body were no longer necessary, as all her bandages had been removed. Now the girl was wearing blue pajamas and sitting up in bed.

After a bit, Dr. Tsurugi took the memo pad in hand and wrote, *How are you feeling?* He handed it to her. He did so because D hadn't bothered to say anything at all.

Scanning the note, Lori nodded. Fidgeting, she adjusted the collar of her pajamas and tugged down the sleeves. She seemed embarrassed to have anyone see the marks her radiation poisoning had left.

Mr. D came to see you, the physician scribbled on the memo pad. *He wants you to get well soon.*

D picked up the pen. On seeing what he wrote on the memo, Dr. Tsurugi's eyes bulged out: *Why did your parents leave town?*

"Wait just one minute," the physician snarled. "This young lady's still a patient undergoing treatment. I didn't bring you here for this. I wanted you to help bring a little life back into her. Most patients need cheering up more than anything. Especially a girl her age."

"And I came here because I have questions," D replied.

"I can't believe your nerve. I never should've brought you here."

"You can cheer her up any time. But my work won't wait."

The physician held his tongue.

D continued, "One of the Nobility has been created through means that are still unclear. If that number is allowed to swell to a hundred, we'll be powerless to stop them. It's my job to get rid of him. But if I had to take out every person in town, that'd be a bit too much of a workload."

"This is insane," the physician said with a mournful sigh.

D turned to face Lori. Silently, he awaited her reply.

Memories flickered in Lori's mind. This was the same question the shadowy figure had put to her the night before. No one cared about her at all. Her parents' experiments were the only thing on anyone's mind. Choking the rage that'd risen to her throat back down again, Lori raised her face. The Hunter's visage greeted her. Cold and veiled in an unearthly aura, his dashing countenance seemed sad nonetheless. The anger vanished from Lori's heart. Putting her left hand over her right so the scars on the back of it couldn't be seen, Lori slowly scratched away with the pen.

I don't know. On our last night in town, as I was walking past the lab, I heard my father tell my mother, "This is going to change the world." Right after that, the two of them headed out somewhere, and while I was sleeping the law came and hauled us off to jail.

"Change it how, I wonder?" Dr. Tsurugi mused. Not saying a word, D looked over his shoulder. Over to the next room. The operating room. The room that had a corpse strapped to the table. The physician's complexion turned the color of clay. "You couldn't possibly mean—"

"I don't know," D said. "But you'd best leave."

"What on earth do you mean?"

"You're better off not knowing."

"You must be joking, after all I've gone through." Dr. Tsurugi added petulantly, "Need I remind you that I was the one who destroyed the vampire last night?"

"I'll see you later."

"But, I—" The physician was about to say something, but he bit his lip. Indignant, he left Lori's sickroom.

D's right hand went into action. *Aside from your family, who went into the lab the most?*

After pausing for a moment, Lori wrote, *Mayor Ming.*

Shining Serpent Pass

CHAPTER 4

I

The following incident took place shortly before D visited the hospital. Taking advantage of her employer's departure for a town meeting, the mayor's maid Nell snuck into the garden. Checking to see that no one else was around, she called out, "Ben!" Her muscular paramour from the cleaners didn't answer. Knitting her brow dubiously, Nell headed over to the base of the massive peach tree that always served as the site of their trysts.

"Boo!" Ben shouted, suddenly poking his head out from behind the tree.

"Oh, Ben, don't scare me like that!" Though relief spread through her heart, an odd sense of incongruity started to gnaw at Nell. Ben didn't quite seem like himself. Sure, his face and his build were the same as ever, but there was something strange about him. Was that an annoying little smirk on his lips?

"What's wrong, Nell? Do I have something stuck on my face or something?" he asked. He sounded just like Ben, too.

Nell shook her head. "It's nothing."

"Oh, really? Then how about a kiss?"

And with that he took Nell in his arms before she could resist and his lips met hers. For a few seconds the two of them stood fused together like a lone pillar by their firm embrace, but soon the strength fled Ben's body. Limp as a wet noodle, he quickly collapsed among the roots of the tree.

Sparing not a glance to the lover who'd so suddenly lost consciousness, Nell scanned her surroundings. Her countenance remained as sensuous as ever, but there was something inexplicably strange about her expression.

"When I saw the young buck here slipping into the mayor's backyard, I had a hunch about what he was up to—and it paid off," Nell said, adding, "I should give this little lady a piece of my mind for screwing around while she's on the clock. Of course, it made my job that much easier, so I'll let it go this time. Lover boy's gonna be out for a while—I'm gonna have to borrow your body, missy."

And then, after dragging her boyfriend's limp form into the cover of the bushes, Nell reclaimed her prim demeanor and returned to the house with a light gait.

On entering the house, Nell quickly locked each and every door. She stood in the middle of the living room with a pensive expression that suggested she was lost in deep thought or grim recollection. But soon she opened her eyes and gave a satisfied nod. "Oh, I see now—there's still another vamp around. And where they're covering this up and making like the girl's not better yet . . . That'd be a D plan, I bet," she laughed.

While the voice was Nell's, the manner was unmistakably that of Pluto VIII. But the real question was, what did he hope to accomplish by inhabiting her boyfriend, then leaping from him to her and rifling through her memories?

"Nothing at all out of the ordinary around the house, she thinks. Hold everything—she's been told not to go into the cellar without asking permission. Bingo! Then I say we go have us a permission-free peek."

Walking softly so Laura wouldn't hear her from the bedroom where she remained in hiding, Nell headed for the cellar door with a shameless grin. It wasn't locked. Pushing the door open, she found a wooden staircase that sank down into the darkness.

Muttering, "Eww, creepy," with unabashed interest, Nell gathered up the hem of her long skirt and slowly stepped into the dark.

Power lines and hot water pipes coming all the way from the industrial sector ran the length and breadth of the ceiling. From the center of the cellar, with its walls lined with wooden crates and jugs of fuel, Nell surveyed her surroundings with a deeply suspicious gaze.

"Well, nothing out of the ordinary here," said the maid. "Now, then, what was the focus of Miss Nell's suspicions . . . " Her eyes, now charged with an eerie gleam, crept along the walls, floor, and ceiling in rapid succession. Before long, they stopped again at her own feet. Coarsely muttering, "Damn, I just don't get it," Nell folded her arms in deliberation. "Any way you slice it, it's just a plain old cellar."

Her eyes began to creep all over the place again, but this time they were infused with an even more tenacious glint. "If I were hiding a switch in the cellar, I'd put it somewhere no one could find it, I reckon."

And, saying that, Nell headed to a corner stacked with empty boxes. "No, I wouldn't—I'd do the exact opposite. The best place a person can hide is in a crowd. And if you had a switch you didn't want anyone to notice, you'd put it where anyone could see it."

Swishing the hem of her skirt, Nell headed over to the control box high on the wall. "As our Miss Nell recalls, she heard strange voices and the creak of gears around here. Meaning . . ." Her sharp eyes stared at a row of nearly a dozen levers. "Maybe it's this one, the least grimy of the lot . . . " Grabbing one in the middle of the row, Nell gave it a twist to the right. With a harsh creaking, just as the maid recalled, there was the sound of gears meshing.

"Whoa!"

As Nell cried out, her body swung about in a circle. To be more precise, she was turned completely around when the spot she was standing on pivoted away easily and revealed a circular hole. A wooden ladder stretched down into a darkness far deeper than the gloom of the cellar.

"So, this must be what made our Miss Nell so suspicious. Don't worry, dear. Uncle Pluto will find the answers for you now," she chortled.

Eyes glittering wildly, Nell went over to the ladder. Checking that no one else was around, she headed down into the new, lower cellar. The ladder was sturdy enough, but the smoothness of the rungs clearly suggested someone had been making frequent use of it for decades now. Fifty rungs down, she reached the bottom.

"Let's see. A switch, a switch . . ." Groping in the dark, her hand soon struck a wall. Finding a small switch, she flicked it on.

A feeble light swelled in the darkness. There lay an area so vast it almost seemed as if the whole town would fit inside it. In the very center of that chamber rested a lone box of an unmistakable nature. Though its surface was free of ornamentation, it was clearly a coffin.

Anxiously muttering, "It's still morning," to herself, Nell started walking toward the coffin. "Hard to believe the mayor of all people would be keeping a monster in his cellar."

As she reached for the coffin's lid without hesitating, someone grabbed Nell by the hair. She started to scream, but, before she could finish, her neck was slashed wide open. Bright blood splashed across the floor.

And, at that very instant, there was a most bizarre incident in another part of town. A short while earlier, a carpenter had discovered a squat man sleeping in the woods. Or at least he'd decided the man was sleeping after checking him for a pulse, but, by the time several other townsfolk and the people from the law enforcement bureau had arrived, his opinion had changed. He now believed it to be a corpse. After all, while the man's heart was still beating, he wasn't breathing at all. When it became known the body was that of the outsider who'd accompanied the gorgeous Vampire Hunter, the site was surrounded by a squawking throng.

"Why on earth—?"

"Went and killed himself. Must've wanted to get even with us for not making him feel welcome in town."

"And I keep telling you even though I seen him mixing it up with the locals in my saloon, he just didn't seem the type to do himself in."

"Heart's beating but he ain't breathing none," one of the onlookers noted. "What good can come of that, I ask you?"

"Good question," said someone from the law enforcement bureau. "At any rate, we'll have to put him out of his misery, right?"

"Right you are," said one of the townsfolk with a nod. "Good riddance, I say. Finish him off!"

"Will do," one of the lawmen said. Drawing an enormous automatic handgun from his holster, he pointed it at Pluto VIII's head. The surrounding mob hustled back out of range. And then, just as the public servant was about to pull the trigger, the man leapt up, fresh as a daisy. With a startled cry, the lawman flinched away.

"You damn idiots! I ain't on display here!" the squat sleeper bellowed. Looking around contemptuously and seeing how the crowd of townsfolk watched him from a safe distance, he spat, "You people are pathetic. You don't have the faintest clue what kind of crazy shit your trusty leader keeps for a pet, but you'll stand around and watch someone who collapsed in the street get their brains blown out."

Needless to say, the foul-tempered man was Pluto VIII, having returned to his own body the instant his host Nell was slain.

†

Shortly after D watched Lori write the mayor's name, the Hunter left the hospital. Dr. Tsurugi requested that he stay and talk with the girl a while longer, but D replied that business came first. Stepping out the door, D was surrounded by three figures. Sheriff Hutton and two deputies—the very same people he'd gone to see at the law enforcement bureau earlier. All of them were wearing gun belts.

"Figured you'd be here, creep," the sheriff snarled, rocket launcher in one hand. The other two held shotguns at the ready.

Seeing their weapons leveled at his heart, D asked, "You have some business with me?" His tone was languid. He was standing in full sunlight. For a creature like a dhampir, descending in part from the Nobility, the conditions couldn't be worse for doing battle.

"You wanna know if we got business? What did you think, we came here to take you out for a drink?" said one of the deputies. "For a freakin' outsider, you got some nerve. I don't care if you're a dhampir or whatever the hell you are—you're out of line. We're gonna give you a nice, long lesson in what happens when you threaten the sheriff in this town."

"I've got a full day tomorrow before my time's up. Can't this wait until then?"

"Are you nuts?! We let a little bastard like you take care of our trouble here, and me and my boys won't look like we're worth our pay no more." Gouts of flame seemed to shoot from Sheriff Hutton's eyes. His rocket launcher was set to discharge all its chambers in a single shot. He had only to push the button, and seven pencil missiles would blast the beautiful Hunter into unrecognizable scraps.

Seeing that a fight was unavoidable, D asked softly, "Are we going to do this here?"

"Now, that's what I like to hear. I'm impressed you ain't trying to make a run for it. Of course, we're still gonna make you pay for coming off so damn tough," the older of the two deputies muttered, swinging the end of his shotgun to indicate an alley that was dark even by daylight.

Meeting the flames of hatred focused on him like a blowtorch with his ever-frosty demeanor, D asked, "Ready to make your move?"

"You first."

Each standing ten feet away, the two deputies braced their shotguns. They'd taken up positions they calculated to be well beyond the reach of D's longsword. No matter what move he might try to make, their shotguns should prove faster than his sword. Their guns already had the first shell in the chamber. The tension was rising by the second.

A lone invader ivy bush grew from the ground by D's feet. Because it had an amazing knack for propagation, exterminating this weed was of the utmost importance, but efforts toward that end never went well. Every time someone thought they had it beat, it would put forth a new shoot within three days, if even part of its fine root structure remained, and it took less than three weeks for it to reach maturity. Though it had no blossoms, it displayed the greatest determination to live and had spread everywhere from the colder regions to the greener belts. D's right hand reached for one of its branches. It was a graceful movement that kept the tense lawmen from putting any more pressure on their trigger fingers. Effortlessly snapping the plant off at its root, D waved it at the men like a great green wad of cotton candy. "Come on."

"You got it!" they shouted, squeezing the triggers with the brute strength their delight lent them. With the gravest of roars, each weapon released three dozen pellets—seventy-two balls of shot loosed in a sheath of flame at D's chest. One can't help but wonder if the two men saw the flash of green that seemed to sweep the hot lead away a split second before it was due to strike. Tiny lead balls plunked down on the crushed stone road, and the two deputies felt the chill of the blade sinking into their skulls. Surely neither of them would've believed he could use the invader ivy leaves and branches to knock the flying buckshot out of the air.

Still brandishing his bloodstained sword, D said to the rocket-launcher-packing giant, "Come on."

The giant trembled. The murderous implement under his arm had become a mere chunk of iron that offered no security at all. What guarantee did he have that a man who could knock buckshot out of the air with a branch couldn't turn his own missiles back on him? Imagining himself caught in a burning white flash that would reduce him to bloody chunks sailing through the air, the sheriff grew pale.

"How about it?" the Hunter said. "You've already got your weapon out."

Hutton had no choice but to go through with it. But no matter what weapon he had, he didn't think it would save him from the Hunter's sword. The sheriff felt the Grim Reaper brushing the nape of his neck.

At that moment, Dr. Tsurugi came running into the alley in great haste. Instantly realizing what was going on, he stepped between the two of them and turned to D. "Please, just stop," the physician said. "There's been entirely too much killing already. If you kill the sheriff, then you really will have to leave here. Even the mayor couldn't do anything about it."

D's hand went into action, easily shoving the physician aside. The fight had already begun, and D's sword had been drawn. It wouldn't be going back in its sheath until it'd tasted the blood of all who made themselves his foe.

The sheriff's Adam's apple bobbed as he swallowed loudly. For the first time, it dawned on him just who he'd chosen to go up against.

The stir of excited voices suddenly hung in the air over town. "Sheriff! Sheriff!" a voice cried, and there was the sound of approaching footsteps.

"You're a lucky man." Giving a light wave of his right hand that threw every last drop of gore from his blade to the ground, D walked right by the frozen sheriff's side. He simply left, as if saying he was finished with the lawman. And in the Hunter's place, a deputy came running into the alley. Seeing the carnage, he froze in his tracks.

"Wha—what do you want?!" the sheriff stammered.

No sooner had he asked the question than the ground shook terribly. No earthquake could even begin to compare to this. It felt like the earth itself had shifted nearly ninety degrees. Panic swept over the people. The crying of children echoed from more than one home.

"What on earth's going on?" This time it was the physician who shouted the question.

"It's Magnetic Storm Pass."

"That's impossible. We're not supposed to be headed south-southwest!"

"Yeah? Well, we are!"

Frightened screams and angry shouts bounced across the shifting earth as it continued to rock wildly. Ahead of the moving town, the entrance to a narrow pass formed by the slopes of a pair of mountains was visible, and a purple cloud could be seen masking that entrance. That magnetic field would wreak havoc with anything electronic, and the town was headed straight for it.

So, what exactly was the Magnetic Storm Pass? Simply put, it was another slice of insanity spawned by a dispute between Nobles. At the end of an interminable battle over the borders of their domain, one Noble faction had set various offensive and defensive devices along the perimeter of what they held was their land. They built a spatial distortion that could pack infinity into a finite area and swallow any invaders. They made visible light into a weapon that could slice through the solid steel hull of a flying battleship. They constructed illusion projectors that not only made people see things, but could even convince them they were part of an entirely different ecosystem. And finally, they created a magnetic storm with the power to disrupt the electrical systems of any machine. Though the Nobility that created these defenses were dying out, the weapons, fed by nuclear power sources, continued to terrorize humanity. And it was one such deadly device that had its lair in the very pass the town was now rushing toward.

"That's odd . . . the warnings aren't sounding."

"Warnings be damned. There's no way in hell our route should be taking us through there!" a voice bellowed angrily out on streets where darkness and light intermingled seductively.

Purple bolts of lightning zipped down the lightning rods. The string of small explosions that could be heard were most likely from circuit breakers that could no longer bear the load. Now, blackness claimed the heavens and earth, and tendrils of light like colossal serpents surrounded the entire town. Factory shutters rattled down noisily, and the radiating fins spread wide on the electrical discharge towers. Energy absorption rods began extending from the ship's sides.

"What's wrong with the navigational computers?" shouted someone in the underground control room.

"There's nothing wrong with the computers," another voice replied shrilly.

"But we're way off course!"

"Someone put in bad data, I tell you!"

"Damn it! Who in blazes could've done that?!"

†

Grains of sand and small pebbles struck D and Dr. Tsurugi's cheeks.

"This doesn't look good. Doctor, you'd better hurry home."

"Come to mention it, so should you," the young physician replied.

"It's a long way back to my quarters."

"I'll walk you there."

D looked at the physician's face. And then he casually started to walk away. Dr. Tsurugi followed right behind him.

Lightning raced across the earth. Thin, wriggling threads of it. Spraying sand, flinging stones, the lightning wrapped around a gatepost and gave off a shower of sparks. The dazzling display of light made D look like white-hot metal. Along the town's sides, the energy absorption rods were also catching the lightning. It would be sent to the nuclear reactors via transformers. Tasting untold bounty for the first time in ages, the reactors showed their satisfaction with their rising, pale blue flames.

D continued silently down the street. Serpents of light raced all around him, raising their heads menacingly at the hem of his coat and spitting fire.

"I'm going back," the physician said from behind him. "Not because I'm getting scared or anything. Oh, I'm scared, all right. But I realized at present we really can't afford to have me getting hurt."

D nodded.

Bowing and excusing himself, the physician did an about-face. Just above him, there was a flash of silvery light. A bolt of lightning that was about to strike his head was split in half, and the fragments twitched on the ground. Completely oblivious to what had happened, Dr. Tsurugi raced off.

Again the town shook. A phosphorescent flash engulfed an electrical discharge tower, and flames shot from its base. Flashes of electricity zipped from the ground in the industrial sector. The energy absorption circuits had surpassed their capacity. Absorption and discharge—both methods had reached their limits.

D had noticed that the town's course had changed. There was no way a navigation system governed by a number of computers working in concert would plot a course that took them right through the middle of a magnetic storm. Some outside agent had adjusted it. But why? Where on earth were they taking the town? Those were questions best put to the mayor.

D stopped in his tracks. A man staggered from the path that ran beside a house. He was clutching at his throat. This was no victim of electrocution. D's eyes glittered at the sight of his oddly pale skin. Turning around, D went to cross the street. The man collapsed on the spot.

An especially massive electricity snake wriggled down the street. D sprinted. The shining serpent sank into the man's midsection. Black smoke rose from him, and the stench of burning flesh pervaded the area. His charred corpse rolled into the street.

Lightning coursed at D from all sides, only to be sundered by silvery flashes.

As D was about to take a step forward, the smoking black mass suddenly moved. Bracing himself with his arms, he slowly raised his torso. Needless to say, his hair and clothes were singed, and his face was burnt to a crisp. Bits of sizzled cloth and hair rained down on the road. The man was getting up.

There weren't many creatures that could be jolted with fifty thousand volts and not be the worse for wear. The Nobility was one of them. It seemed this man was infected with the disease.

A red cavity opened in the lower half of the blackened face. His mouth. That alone was as red as ever, as if to offer some contrast to his pearly white fangs. How does a person charred to a crisp get to their feet? Burnt body framed with white light, he slowly began walking toward D. Smoke wafted from his limbs. Probing bolts of lightning crackled from his singed flesh.

D didn't move a muscle. A blackened hand reached for him. A second before it closed on the Hunter's throat, the hand swept away in an elegant arc and then fell back to earth. D seemed to listen for the *thunk* of it hitting the ground.

The charred human form began to lose its thickness, turning into a pile of dust. In the blink of an eye, the gusting winds had scattered the remains far and wide. This was the second case of the vampire infection. However, simply just because a person had turned into a vampire didn't necessarily mean they would crumble like ash when true death claimed them. The degree of corruption their body manifested depended entirely on how long it'd been since they'd been made a servant of the Nobility. A person who'd spent three days in their service would leave a rotting corpse. Given two weeks, the flesh would melt from their bones. If more than a year had passed, then they might be reduced to dust. In death alone they would be bound by the same rules as the living. What'd just occurred to the corpse of this vampirized individual simply wasn't possible. Or was this a case where his transformation into one of the Nobility had long been concealed? No, that wasn't possible, either. This was an entirely new disease. Perhaps it should've been called Nobilitation Syndrome.

D turned his back on the remains and started to walk away. But the question remained: where was he headed?

II

The town's ability to insulate itself from the storm had reached its limits. Breakers in four of the five electrical discharge towers had burnt out from the overload, and the remaining tower was down to fifty percent effectiveness.

"Nuclear reactor number one—energy level at fifty-two percent over normal capacity."

"Number two is fifty-seven percent over. She's got all she can handle."

"Number three is sixty-nine percent over—well into the danger zone. Danger! Danger! Danger!"

"Navigational control room, how many minutes more until we're clear of the magnetic storm?" Mayor Ming asked.

"We can't be certain. According to our data, this magnetic belt is approximately 2.95 miles wide. At our present speed, that'd be 5 minutes, 19.6 seconds."

"Report what degree of danger the town would face in that five minutes if we were to shut down energy absorption for one, two, or all three of our reactor towers."

"If all three towers are shut down—town will be destroyed in 2 minutes and 22 seconds. Two towers—town will be destroyed in 3 minutes and 5.4 seconds. One tower—town will be destroyed in 5 minutes and 21.3 seconds."

"Keep only the number one reactor in operation. Increase cruising speed to twenty-five miles per hour."

"That's insane. The outer shell will suddenly be taking three times as much voltage—it'll blow the reactor!"

"I realize it's crazy," the mayor said. "But we can't do a damn thing unless we get clear of this storm!"

"Roger that."

The instant the other two nuclear reactors stopped absorbing power, the remaining energy turned at once on the number one reactor, snapping at it like the fangs of a crazed beast. Fire shot from the energy flow control system and five of the safeties, and the now unbalanced flames of nuclear fusion quickly drove the needle toward the danger zone. In no time at all, pale blue flames had burst through the bottom plates of the town and were shooting wildly into the air.

†

Wracked by the powerful shocks, Lori gave a silent scream and clung desperately to her bed. Dr. Tsurugi ran to her. Shouting Lori's name, he threw himself at her and pulled her tight to him. Lori clung to his warm chest. The physician's heart kept pounding wildly. *He's just as scared as I am*, Lori thought. For the first time, she found herself feeling something other than curiosity toward the young doctor.

†

Ahead of the town, there wriggled a particularly large and fierce serpent of light. Lightning crackled from every inch of it, and when bolts from it brushed the craggy cliffs to either side of it, the surface was fused into glass or rained down on the town. Chunks of rock crashed through the roof of a house somewhere, and a woman could be heard screaming. A compressor in one of the factories took a hit as well, turning the braided steel air hose into a high-voltage cable that whipped into workers' bodies and scalded their faces. White light engulfed the town. Silicon polymer roofs were being blown off houses, and whole trees were being sucked up into the sky, roots and all. People scrambled into their basements for protection.

The fierce suction assailed D as well. His traveler's hat and the hem of his coat began to rise. Securing the hat's wide brim with his left hand, D drew his sword with his right. Turning the blade over, he drove it into the earth. Kneeling, he waited. Pebbles flew up, and roofing materials followed right after them.

†

The true mayhem was concentrated in the reactor and navigation control centers. A serpent of light that slipped in through a fresh hole in the wall thrashed ruthlessly through the bulkhead, flinging workers everywhere. The pungent odor of burnt flesh filled the air. Snagging a flying worker with one hand, the mayor slammed him back against the floor. The old man's strength was incredible. Raising his voice, he asked, "Can't correct our computers, am I right?"

"No, it's no use!"

"Then switch to manual controls!" Mayor Ming snapped back.

"Manual controls on these were scrapped over five hundred years ago."

The mayor's face took on the fierceness of a demon. Pulling the serpent of light that was devastating his surroundings to his chest, the mayor tore it apart with his bare hands. Black smoke rose from his hands and his torso. His hair stood on end, and lightning leapt around in his mouth. "Where the hell are we going?" he said. "Who's doing this, and where do they think they're taking my town?"

†

D heard the riot of life and death all around him. Kneeling, gripping the sword he'd driven into the earth, he looked like an obsidian statue. With all the elements howling furiously around him, he alone remained unaffected. Light filled the air above him. A serpentine form twice as thick as any man could get his arms around was dropping toward D, scorching the air molecules as it went. Here was the leader of this deadly swarm. Never breaking his pose, D flew backward. Passing him in midair, the serpent fell to the ground and broke in half before taking to the air once again.

†

T he magnetic belt is pulling away from the town."
"Pull out of it at full speed."
As if in response to that joyful cry, blue-black space stretched across the forward view screen—a sky sealed in tranquil darkness, without a hint of blinding light. As if beaten off by the winds gusting against them, the lights coloring the town began to fall off behind them.

"We're clear!" someone shouted. Cheers suddenly filled the air.

†

W hen Sheriff Hutton called on Ming, some three hours had passed since the mayor had left one of the workers in charge of overseeing the removal of the radioactive waste. The sheriff found Ming settled into a chair in his private chambers. "How are the townsfolk?" the mayor asked in ill humor, his eyes shut.

"They're finally settling down. We're looking into the number of injured now," the sheriff said in a tone that sounded somewhat intrigued.

"Then, I gather there were no fatalities?"

"Yeah. Surprisingly few wounded, too. Hard to believe no one got electrocuted. Radiation poisoning's been pretty minor, to boot."

"We have that medicine I came up with forty years ago to thank for that. Anyway, what do you want?" The mayor opened his eyes. Somewhat reproachfully, he added, "You ought to still be out there."

"Actually, I've come to gab about old times with you," the sheriff said, smiling at him. The mayor had never seen him smirk like that. "You happen to remember Ende Remparts? He was a twelve-year-old kid."

The expression that formed on the mayor's face was that of an entirely different person. "Just what the hell do you think you're doing?!"

"Poor kid had a muscular disease they could've treated well enough in a town on the ground, but you hated the idea of anyone getting off. Told him the condition was untreatable, and he ended up offing himself as a result, didn't he?"

"Hey!"

"How about that time with Ebenezer Villzuya?" the sheriff continued, stroking the barrel of his rocket launcher. "That one I had a hand in. We were in the middle of a famine, and he stole a half-pound more synthetic butter than he was supposed to get. His kids were on the brink of starving. The rest of the town pretended not to notice. After all, no one else was half as bad off as his family. Why, even you were pretty easy on him at first. But in the end, you just couldn't find it in you to let the first man to break the rules in the town you made get away with it. So, this cuss here, who was just a deputy at the time, went in and gunned down his whole family, then made it look like suicide."

The mayor got up out of his chair and barked, "Who the hell are you?!"

"It's me. Take a good look now. I'm the one and only Sheriff Hutton. Given name: Bailey Hutton; height: nine feet nine inches;

weight: five hundred thirty-five pounds; place of birth: three hundred thirty-fourth sector of the Eastern Frontier. I first came on board . . . "

A loud crack resounded at his jaw. The massive frame of five hundred and thirty-five pounds lurched backward and rolled on the floor. Dashing over, the mayor was just about to stomp his right foot down on the giant's throat when the barrel of the rocket launcher rose from the floor to stop him.

"Hey, now—cut that out. I don't care how tough you are. Seven blasts from this will send you straight to the hereafter," the sheriff said, rubbing his jaw as he got back up. He was like a walking mountain. If someone had opened the door just then, they wouldn't have seen anything besides his back. On the other hand, the mayor stood only five foot eight and weighed less than a hundred and fifty pounds. Though nutritional supplements might've helped to explain how he'd lived to be over two hundred, the punch he'd just delivered was beyond anything imaginable. "Ow, that smarts. You pack more of a wallop than I'd heard," the sheriff said as he nursed his jaw, but his voice was clearly that of another person.

"Oh, it's *you*? Got one hell of a strange power there," the mayor said, not seeming particularly upset as he went back to his chair. He must've figured that as long as he knew what and whom he was dealing with, he could do away with them whenever he pleased. "I thought you were a bit of a shady character from the moment I heard you were D's partner—and then you go off possessing our sheriff and stealing his memories. Well, what exactly do you intend to do next?"

"Nothing serious, really. Compared to what a heavyweight scoundrel like you gets away with, what I'm asking for is small potatoes."

"I see. And that would be?"

"I want what the Knights left you."

"Really?"

"I've been over every inch of that house, and I couldn't find a thing. From what they told me, it seems you wanted it, too. In which case, it's pretty obvious where it'd have to be now."

"Unfortunately, I don't know its location either." Sitting there in his chair, the mayor spread his hands in a display of innocence. "When I found out you tried to save them, I very much wanted to ask you exactly the same thing."

"I see. So, you were the one behind that whole little act about bringing me in for stealing some flowers?" the sheriff said in Pluto VIII's voice, grinning at him as the biker would. "Too bad about that. But, you see, I've got no proof what you're telling me is true. Worse yet, your town's got these vampires running around and no one knows when the hell they got on. *Got on . . .* " he snorted. "That's a laugh. Of course no one would know when. They've *been here* since the very beginning, after all."

The voice suddenly became that of the sheriff. "Six months back, on your orders, I snatched Dumper Griswell and Yan Will. Didn't have the foggiest notion what you intended to use them for, but no one in town was gonna miss a couple of worthless drunks. But with things as they are now, I kinda have to wonder—did them two maybe get themselves turned into vampires?"

"And just what would you do if they did?" the mayor said menacingly.

"Hey, now! I thought I told you not to move. Besides, trying to do anything to me won't accomplish anything. Your sheriff here's the one who'll take the lumps, while I'll just go back to my old body and slip into someone else. Hell, I could even use your own daughter . . . "

"And could you move into another body from the one you're in now?" the mayor asked.

"Yep."

"Hmm. Then maybe you ought to try possessing me. That way you'll know straight away whether I'm telling the truth or not."

"Wow, knock me over with a feather. Are you sure about this? I'll be privy to your every little secret."

"I don't mind a bit. After all, this way, you'll see it'd be in your interest to join forces with me for a little while."

"Join forces?"

"That's right. We're both after the same thing, but there are any number of ways it might be used."

"Ah, I see. So, as long as your use and mine don't conflict, we'd be fine. Good enough."

"What'll you do about the sheriff?"

"I'll screw with his brain a bit and leave him snoozing. Make sure no one comes in here for a while."

The mayor spoke into his intercom, saying something to the effect that no one was to be let into his chambers. He turned to face the sheriff. One of the giant's hands latched onto his deeply wrinkled wrist. Two seconds passed . . . then three . . . And then, with a crash that shook the whole room, five hundred and thirty-five pounds of lawman fell over like a tree. An expression of amazement that wasn't his at all quickly formed on the mayor's face as he sat there with his eyes shut.

"I . . . I can't believe that." The voice that slipped from his dry lips was choked with fear. Almost as if his own thoughts terrified him . . . "Who could do such an awful thing . . . And you still call yourself—or should I say myself—human?!"

Lari

CHAPTER 5

I

Though the crisis had passed, the town showed signs that
it hadn't yet recovered from the tragedy. The owners of
devastated houses didn't look very motivated to repair the
damage as they sat around sulking, and their neighbors didn't
seem at all inclined to help cheer them up. Every face wore a
demented expression, and the people stood around like empty
husks, or milled about in the streets aimlessly. It was almost as if
the overwhelming disaster had stripped everything that mattered
from them. But in the midst of the milling townsfolk, mixed with
the chatter of the frantically scrambling relief party that answered
directly to the mayor, a crisp and spirited young voice rang out. It
was that of Dr. Tsurugi, working at the emergency medical facility
that'd been established in front of the hospital. "Okay," he said,
"I want you to form a single file—no pushing—and one by one,
take a seat."

Once a patient was seated in the simple revolving chair,
Dr. Tsurugi ran his hands over their clothed form and asked
them a few questions. The palms of his gloves were imprinted
with some kind of medical diagnostic program. The questions
were to gauge the level of mental upheaval each patient
had suffered.

"Okay—Point nine seven. A slight case of radiation poisoning. Mental balance is . . . no problem. Pick your medicine up over there. Okay, next!"

Only at the very end did a bit of honest emotion slip into the doctor's face, but shortly thereafter he reclaimed his beaming countenance. It was a sight to see him in action, working through the endless chain of patients at a rate of less than a minute each. However, the person by his side dispensing medicine wasn't the nurse. It was a lovely young lady of seventeen who couldn't compliment anyone or say a single word to comfort them, but who showed all the compassion she could muster in her large eyes as she quietly handed them their medicine. It was difficult to believe that, less than ten hours earlier, her whole body had been covered with plasters for removing radioactive contamination. It was Lori.

After seeing how terribly overburdened Dr. Tsurugi was, she'd volunteered to help out. Of course, the physician's situation hadn't been helped by the fact that his nurse had been horribly frightened and had yet to recover from her dementia. As Lori gazed at the townsfolk and the numb expressions they wore, there was sorrow in her eyes, but another, more invigorating feeling filled her slight frame. She'd lost the use of her voice and ears, but she had to go on living. The determination to do so burned strongly in her. However, on a more basic level, the girl was immensely pleased to be able to do something on her own.

Lori's smiling eyes were suddenly infused with an intense glimmer. A powerful figure in black was coming down the same street filled by the lines of townsfolk.

D stopped next to the physician. "Make it through okay?" he asked. From the Hunter's tone of voice it wasn't clear whether he was actually concerned or just being polite. And, of course, the sound of it didn't reach Lori's ears at all. Still, she got the feeling there was something beyond the usual severity in the gaze he cast on the physician and herself, and it made her heart leap.

"I muddled through somehow," Dr. Tsurugi replied. "How about you? I've heard dhampirs have a far greater tolerance for radiation than the average human—" The physician caught himself and quickly bit his lip. A few of the townspeople looked surprised by what they'd heard, but most showed no reaction at all. While the shock of the magnetic storm was to blame, the effect it'd had on the populace was just too great.

"Is the corpse inside?" the Hunter asked.

"Yes, he's still asleep. I don't know what you did to him, but it must've been incredible."

"I'd like a look at it."

"Fine. But I'd like something in return," the physician said, his hands never taking a break from examining patients.

"What's that?"

"Once you're done with that, I'd like you to help me out."

"There's nothing I could do," said D.

"If you've got arms and legs, we've got work for you."

"Okay, if I've got time." And with that uncharacteristic reply, D went through the door.

Lori's sorrowful gaze followed the Hunter. He hadn't so much as acknowledged her presence.

†

On entering the operating room, D took a portable atomic lamp off the shelf and switched it on. A pale flame blazed up around the wick. The body of the man lying on the operating table on the other side of the room was outlined in blue. Twisting the faucet to get the water running, D looked down at his left hand and said, "I've got some soil ready, too, but what would you like first?"

"Don't ask dumb questions," a voice quickly answered. At the same time, a human face complete with eyes and a nose mysteriously surfaced in the palm of the Hunter's hand. Forming a scowl, it said, "You're splitting hairs with all this talk about fire first or water first, when the truth is nothing's been all that tasty lately. After all, I'm the one who's gotta eat them. Oh, my—we've got a nuclear reactor today? That looks positively delicious. None of that alcohol lamp or dried werewolf dung, thank you. That stuff's the worst!"

Taking a handful of dirt from one of his coat's inner pockets, D put it beside the lamp. "Be quick about it," he said. "The corpse should be waking up soon."

"Hmph. Well if it does, you can just put it back to sleep again. Day in and day out, you're always pushing me around."

"Fire or water?" the Hunter asked.

"Hmm, I'll take the dirt."

D held his left hand over the blackish pile. There was the intense squeal of air being drawn in, and the clod of earth broke apart into a powder that was inhaled by the palm hanging over it.

"That tastes awful!" the voice said after sucking up every last grain of dirt. "This soil hasn't known the usual ups and downs, or been part of the natural circle of life, death, and rebirth. It doesn't take its life from the planet. It's just a decoration laid down over steel. You're not gonna be very satisfied with the kind of results you get by feeding me crap like this!"

Without saying a word, D held his left hand up to the atomic flames.

"Sheesh! You dolt. Water's supposed to be next," the voice squawked, but the Hunter didn't move a muscle. Further curses of "freak" and "sadist" soon died out, and the atomic light—as impossible as it sounds—quickly condensed into a single glowing stream that disappeared into D's hand. Or, to be more precise, into the tiny mouth that'd opened in the palm of his hand. And just how voracious was that mouth? Well, the ultracompact reactor the lamp was equipped with was supposed to be enough to power the atomic flame for more than a decade, but in less than two minutes its color faded, it flickered, and finally it went out.

D didn't so much as raise an eyebrow at that bizarre occurrence, but instead put this hand under the spigot in the sink, palm up now. A few minutes later, the voice sputtered, "That's enough," and as it did, D twisted the faucet to shut it off.

"How are you feeling?" D asked. His eyes remained trained on the corpse.

"Well, I'll get by. I suppose I'm a hell of a lot better than I was last night." Along with the words, a gout of flame roared from the palm of the Hunter's hand. In a mouth left pale blue by a few thousand degrees of heat, a red tongue flicked impassively, saying sharply, "So, what the heck do you want analyzed?"

Devoid of pity or any other deeper emotion, D brought his left hand over to the man on the operating table—and put it against his forehead. At that instant, the whole corpse stiffened and bent backward from the waist, like a bow. It snapped into the shape so fiercely that it wouldn't have been strange to hear his hipbones shattering. Countless red points began to form all over his body, along with specks of blood. Had this body, which had supposedly long since ceased to function, begun to have metabolic activity once again? The vivid red spots grew larger and larger, and in no time their surface tension broke and they began to course down the sides of the body, leaving disturbing trails on his flesh. When the first drop hit the operating table, a faint moan escaped from the corpse.

D had his eyes half-closed. What was his hand trying to do? What kind of analysis? What did he hope to learn from this corpse?

†

When the treatment of the townsfolk and the distribution of medicine had finally wound down, Lori quickly looked at the physician. Massaging his hands, Dr. Tsurugi nodded to her. The girl got up and went into the hospital. Talking pains not to tread too loudly, she peeked into the waiting room. There was nobody there.

Was he in the office, or maybe the operating room? It had never even occurred to Lori that D's business there might be with a corpse. Once more, she stepped out into the hall. She decided to try the office.

A few inches away from her, the door to the operating room opened inward. A figure suddenly appeared. A man completely covered in blood.

Lori froze in her tracks, choking back a scream. The man suddenly collapsed in a heap. When Lori saw the other figure that stood behind him, she desperately tried to keep her knees from failing her. She didn't want him to see her do anything stupid. Having lost her voice and hearing, she was damned if she'd lose anything else now.

As the girl tried desperately to steady her footing, D watched her without saying a word. Waiting until she'd gotten her trembling under control, the Hunter grabbed the corpse by the neck and brought it back into the operating room. As they gazed at the blood spilled on the floor, his eyes held a dark tint.

By the time D went back out into the hall, Lori had returned to her senses. She'd always been a brave girl.

"You want something from me?" D asked. He said it out loud.

Lori tried desperately to follow the movements of his lips. Somehow, she managed to read them. She shook her head. She had no business with him. She just thought it would be nice to see him. That was all.

"While you may not be able to get back what you lost, you can learn something new in return," D remarked impassively, almost as if he didn't care what became of Lori. Not understanding exactly what'd been said to her, Lori pursed her lips with grim resolve and tried not to miss anything else. D said to her, "Come with me. We probably don't have much time."

And with that he walked out. Lori followed after him. A smile had risen to her lips. By watching D's cold profile, she understood what he was saying.

"Just where are you two going?" the physician called to them as they came out the front door.

"Where's the highest point in town?" the Hunter asked in return.

"That'd be the hill behind the factories. Why?"

Nodding with satisfaction, D began to walk away. As the two figures walked off down the street, the physician watched them coolly.

†

The damage to Chad Beckly's house had been relatively minor. Fastening a waterproof tarp over a couple of holes that falling rocks had left in the roof, he decided the repairs could wait for another day. They were a family of four. There was Chad, his wife Vera, and their two sons Luke and Simon. Chad's family was extremely concerned about the way he was acting. Ever since he'd come home from the navigational control room, his expression had been one of deep depression. Skipping dinner entirely, as soon as he'd put the sheet over the roof he'd gone straight to bed.

What was troubling Chad was where the town was headed. The new route that'd been programmed into the computers clearly had them headed right for some of the Nobility's ruins. They'd probably be there in less than two days. The question was, what was waiting for them there? Even the mayor said he didn't know. Legend alone had the answer. Graves. And not the kind of Noble resting place ornamented with elaborate crests and guarded by electronic devices. What slumbered there was . . .

Hauling his mind back from its slide into anxiety, Chad tried his best to get to sleep. The wind howled outside his window. Tomorrow, he'd have to get up before dawn and head back to the control room. What on earth was going to happen to the town? Chad's brain was burning with worry. Downstairs, his wife and children were still up and about. So much had happened, they probably couldn't get settled down to rest.

There was a slight sound . . . A rap at the door, perhaps? His wife walked around. The floorboards creaked. He'd have to speak to the mayor about getting them replaced. But who could be out at this hour? There was absolutely no way he was going back to the control room. Someone came in. The door was still open. There was the sound of something falling over. *Did the missus trip over that dang chair again?* he wondered. *Wait a minute—they didn't get back up.*

Footsteps crossed the living room and started up the stairs. Creaking all the while. Must be his wife. Out in the hall now. Still coming. Slowly. Coming this way. The footsteps stopped. Out in front of the boys' room.

Maybe I should go see who it is? he thought. *No, it's just the little woman, of course. Besides, I'm dog-tired.*

The door opened. *Aw, she shouldn't have gone and done that. Hey, that was a scream just now, wasn't it?* More thuds as things fell. Two of them. The door closed. The footsteps were coming closer. Slowly. No hurry . . . They stopped. In front of his bedroom. It couldn't be . . .

There was a knock on his door. Chad remained in bed. The knocking continued, then stopped for a bit—and started again.

Chad got out of bed. Step by step, each one feeling like it was sinking into the carpet, he headed for the door. He didn't want to go. He knew it was his wife outside the door. But what if it wasn't . . .

Right in front of the door, Chad paused for a moment. The knocking stopped. The doorknob clicked as it turned. Gently at first, then quickly . . .

With a tremendous snap, the doorknob, the plate around it, and the section of door they were attached to all vanished. There was a gaping hole now. And the door had swung open. Someone was standing there. It wasn't his wife.

A horrible choking sensation assailed Chad. He reached up to claw at his own throat, but before his hand got there his heart had stopped.

†

While it was indeed a hill, with a height of only about fifteen feet, it hardly had a commanding view. And yet, for one of the two it was surely more than adequate. After all, Lori wasn't alone, and by her side was a man the darkness suited more than anyone. Despite the moonlight, the plains they overlooked were as dark as anything imaginable, but the sky to the east was already laced with the first thin light of dawn. The wind pricked at Lori's cheeks. It was as cold and sharp as an awl. Lori gazed at D while D watched the eastern sky. Did those trapped in darkness hope for the light of dawn, too?

So, what had they come up here to do? D bent down by Lori's side and put one of the fingers of his left hand to the ground. Lori read the words he wrote in the sand. *I hear voices*, D had written. What voices was he talking about? The message seemed almost cruel.

Lori turned up the collar of her coat. The wind tossed her soft hair as it passed. *So cold*, she thought. *Maybe people weren't meant to live out in the wild.* After all, it was this cold even at daybreak.

The town was still moving. But going where? It had no destination. Where was it heading? Not even Lori had any idea what D was thinking about. While it was true she'd been raised in town, she'd also experienced life out in the wilderness. The wilds were just too terrible. The fear inspired by the monstrosities and vicious beasts the Nobility had loosed was still enough that the world would quake at dusk today.

Lori had wanted to go back to the town with all her heart. However, the paradise she'd wanted now seemed so hollow. Lori no longer had words or sounds, which was exactly why she could feel things so much more intensely . . . She thought of working reasonable hours, and having reasonable accommodations, food, and clothing, of having a life that was satisfactory, but not satisfying at the same time. The overwhelming sense of loss from the people after they'd made it through the magnetic storm only served to highlight her feelings. If she hadn't experienced life in the wilderness, she probably would've been just like the rest. Although she was far from conceited, Lori knew there was something wrong with the town as it was now. But, in her silent world of despair, did she have reason to be proud of being different from the rest? An inescapable sense of loneliness filled her little heart. While she had the feeling the world she was meant to live in was just around the next bend, for Lori that was a far-distant land. *If I get off this town, what'll happen then?* she wondered.

To the east, the edges of the mountains had begun to glitter with a rosy hue. Light slipped down the mountainside, becoming a torrent that flooded the plains, and in no time Lori's entire field of view was tinged in gold. She closed her eyes. Even with them closed, she could see. She saw the color of wind. And how the wind shined in its own way.

After a while, D opened his mouth. Lori tried to read his lips. She didn't catch it all. A bit more slowly, D repeated it. Finally she understood him.

Next time, come alone. That's what he was saying.

†

It was a little past six o'clock Morning when D called on the mayor. He found the mayor sleeping in his chair in his office. As a cold pain tightened his chest, the mayor jumped up and saw the Hunter standing by the door. Putting his hand to his throat and breathing a sigh, he asked, "How long have you been there?!"

D said nothing.

"So, it seems I have you to thank for scaring the daylights out of me . . . Just having a dhampir around seems to be enough to give folks nightmares."

"I'm here because I need to ask you something."

"Ah, yes, that's right . . . You were by a little earlier, weren't you? You'll have to excuse me. I was out at the time."

"It seems you had the Knights detained."

The Hunter's softly spoken words made Mayor Ming's eyes bulge. "Who told you that?"

"It doesn't matter. Why did you stop them? Why'd you have them thrown in jail?"

"Do I have to answer that? The only thing you're here to do is to kill our vampire."

"And what if someone manufactured that vampire?" D asked.

"What?!"

"What did the man who boarded your town two centuries ago have to say to you?"

The mayor greeted the question with silence.

"What did it involve?"

More silence. Beads of sweat appeared on the mayor's brow. "Just what I told you before," the mayor finally said.

His voice lacked strength of will, and D shattered it with his own soft tone. "What did the man who visited here two hundred years ago tell you? I can imagine what it was, but I won't mention it. However, it was the Knights who accomplished what your visitor hoped to do. But only after long years had passed. That's what you wanted. What did you want it for? Why did you have a falling-out with the Knights?"

Nothing from the mayor.

"After two centuries, vampires suddenly start showing up here, and yet we can't find the cause for it. There's no one here sucking people's blood and turning people into vampires. There's only one answer—they were manufactured. Made that way by somebody's special process." D's eyes looked like they could suck the soul from the mayor. "Made with the technique he gave to you, and you taught to the Knights. What was in their house?"

Bracing both hands on the head of his cane, the mayor hung his head. "Peace must be maintained in town for all time." A voice closer to a groan flowed from beneath the mayor's bowed head. "The conditions now are ideal. But we're still hounded by destruction and the creatures of nightmare. The mayor has a duty to protect the townsfolk."

"Peace and ideals," D muttered. Coming from his lips, the words lost all meaning and became mere sounds.

"This town is what the Frontier would be ideally." Saying this, the mayor lifted his face. It was warped. His lustrous skin had surely been artificially augmented. The ugly wrinkles that crept across his cheeks looked like furrows in a freshly plowed field. "To live serenely out in the untamed forces of nature without fear of the Nobility or their despicable ilk—that was the human ideal. When I formed this town and peopled it with a select few, I believed I'd gotten closer to that goal than anyone. But many threats still remained. It was still far from perfect . . . "

The mayor's finger pressed the top of his desk. Suddenly, D was in the middle of town. It was the residential section immediately after the magnetic storm. The images must've been shot with a holographic camera. The plastic roofs of many houses were melted, and the electrical discharge towers gave off pale smoke and spat sparks in their death throes. People with burns either hobbled along on their own or were held up by family as they tottered slowly down the street, most likely headed to the hospital. A little girl passed right through D's waist and disappeared into a back room. A fire engine ran over a sofa, then plowed through someone's front door. Fires were springing up everywhere. A middle-aged man grabbed an electrified handrail, lurching backward as purple light shot from him. It was a ghastly tableau.

"This is the town at its limits. A mere magnetic field can't even begin to compare to the other monstrosities the Nobility loosed on the world. Yet, if running into it wreaked this kind of havoc, then what the town considers ideal is still far shy of what I have in mind."

"And making those ideals a reality involves making sacrifices and taking certain steps, doesn't it?" the Hunter said. "Certain bloody steps, I'd say. What exactly did you ask the Knights to do?"

The mayor swallowed loudly. He didn't suppose D was going to leave now, and he wasn't the kind to be taken in by a lie. As Ming was about to slowly take a step, his foot froze in place. An unearthly aura was filling the room. *So this is what a dhampir can do?* he thought. *This is the man called D?* So terrified it wouldn't have been strange if his heart had stopped, too scared to even shake, the mayor gazed at the Hunter's gorgeous countenance.

"Answer me. What did you ask the Knights to do? What did they discover?"

"It was . . . " the mayor panted. An incredibly powerful essence threatened to crush his psyche. "It was . . . "

At that very moment, the intercom on the mayor's desk flashed red. With the series of short, tension-filled buzzes, D's unearthly aura dissipated almost immediately. Wiping at his greasy sweat, the mayor grabbed the intercom microphone. "What is it?"

"This is the navigational control room. We've got a lone flying object approaching from north-northwest at a range of forty miles. Speed is sixty miles per hour. The object is—roughly the same size as our town. We're trying to hail it, but haven't gotten an answer."

"I see. I'll be right there. Don't forget to prepare for a counterstrike, just in case." When he switched off the intercom, the mayor had a relieved look on his face. He felt more at ease having some unknown intruder threatening the town than he did sitting in the same room with the young Hunter. "Guess I'll be going, then," the mayor said without looking in D's direction. Just then the intercom buzzed loudly again.

"What now?"

"The flying object has launched missiles. Three in all. They're approaching now—twenty seconds to impact."

"Get the barrier up!"

"It was damaged by the magnetic field—repairs are still under way."

"Begin firing antiballistic missiles and antiaircraft guns!" When the mayor raised his now pale face once again, he saw no trace of D.

†

The Grim Reaper was winging his way toward the town. A trio of long, thin reapers, actually, with sensors in their tips and flames gushing from the nozzles to their rear. Taking into account their own speed and that of the town, they were constantly adjusting their course to the target as they closed in on it at full speed.

†

At the sight of the Hunter in black who'd appeared without a sound, everyone in the energy output control room forgot their approaching death and stood in a daze.

"Where's the barrier projector?" D asked softly. Even knowing that death was drawing ever nearer, he still managed to maintain his detached tone of voice.

The eyes of all the workers focused on one corner in the back. D headed over to the silver cylinder. He was like a sprinting shadow. Saying not a word, the workers stepped to either side. In the gap they left was a gaping hole where a riot of pale blue electromagnetic waves danced chaotically. There was only one man who didn't leave his post. Welding gear in hand, his body unexpectedly flew backward into the room. Fire rose from the protective plates on his chest. He'd just taken a blast of electromagnetism. Silently, D stood between the man and the rough hole. His handsome face shone blue and cold.

"Don't bother. Can't turn off the electromagnetic wave output," the man shouted as he used his hand to beat out the flames on his chest. "There's a hundred thousand volts running through there. Without a protector on, we're talking instant death."

"Get in touch with the control room," D ordered the frozen workers. "When you need the barrier, I'll send the current through."

Asking no questions, and offering no arguments, the men nodded. One, who appeared to be in charge, brought his mouth over to the microphone on his shoulder, and had them patch him through to the navigational control room.

A slight tremor passed through the ship's hull. The anti-aircraft fire had started. While the town was equipped with antigravity generators and an electronic barrier, their armaments were incredibly primitive. Aside from the Prometheus cannon—which, in a cruel trick of fate, had been stripped down for inspection an hour earlier—they had only twenty high-angle machine cannons with a two-inch bore and thirty antiballistic missile launchers. Of course, they couldn't be expected to produce their own shells and missiles, so those were procured from flying merchants who specialized in dealing with floating cities like theirs. Even so, such merchants were few and far between, meeting the town only three times a year. If they ran out of goods they couldn't produce in the interim, a floating city had no choice but to find them on their own. Many of the battles between two floating cities had resulted from this mutual need. But the hostile actions of the unidentified flying object firing upon them were nothing short of indiscriminate slaughter.

Prismatic flames spread across the sky, and black smoke enveloped the area. To increase their destructive power, the shells for the machine cannons contained depleted uranium and were armed with proximity fuses. Even if they failed to score a direct hit, they would automatically detonate if their sensors detected a target within their destructive range. Each time the big guns fired, the whole town rocked wildly.

The incoming missiles displayed the most astounding behavior. Like sentient beings, they dodged shells and adjusted their speed as they rushed steadily closer. They seemed to be mocking the town.

Minute course adjustments were nearly impossible for the town's antiballistic missiles. Every one that'd been launched left an ineffectual trail of white through the empty sky as it disappeared.

A small, black shadow of death clung to the town. People looked out their windows at the three points of approaching light. On every face was a despondent expression. The thought of the fate those missiles held for them robbed them of their willpower. Long spared the threats of the world below, the fragility of their peace had been made evident by their enemy's attack.

†

M issiles closing—three seconds to impact!" came the bloodcurdling news from the microphone on the man's shoulder. All eyes were on D. The Hunter reached into the hole in the wall, and, grabbing a fistful of cables, he pulled down. From his shoulder to his wrist, pale blue electromagnetic waves clung to him like a spider's web, and white smoke rose from his body. His face didn't show the slightest hint of pain. His right hand went into action, pulling out the ends of the severed cords. Electromagnetic waves covered D entirely . . . Perhaps it was the first time this young man had worn a color other than black. Using his body as a conductor, energy suddenly shot from the reactor to the barrier projector.

Richly colored blossoms opened near the town. Flames that could get as hot as fifty million degrees and a lethal dose of electromagnetic waves and radiation churned through the atmosphere, threatening to destroy the electronic wall that'd suddenly appeared.

The people saw the electromagnetic waves running from D's right hand to his left in reverse direction. D's eyes narrowed. The flow changed back again. The barrier didn't fade until the trio of blasts dissipated in the air.

II

Even after D had backed away, no cheer went up in the control room. What they'd just witnessed was so incredible it left them absolutely stunned with amazement. Their amazement, along with their overwhelming sense of relief, was enough to throw them into a state of dementia. The man before them—their savior—clearly couldn't be human. That's why he was so good-looking.

Lightly tossing his head, D shook off the white smoke still rising from his body.

"The flying object is closing," a somewhat listless voice announced through the microphone. The main craft still remained.

Braced, perhaps, for the next attack, D didn't move.

"It's closing on us—just a thousand yards off, nine hundred, seven hundred, six hundred . . ."

"It's gonna hit us . . ." someone muttered.

"We can't change our heading."

"We've had it now . . ."

A black wind fluttered by the men.

D exited the control room. Racing up the stairs, he charged across the street. The center of town was completely empty. With sunlight falling in a bright shower, the town was a picture of tranquility. A voice he knew cried out, and D looked over his shoulder. Lori and Dr. Tsurugi were dashing toward him. D didn't stop for them, but kept on running. Something became visible beyond the town's defensive walls. The form of their foe was clear now.

It seemed that floating cities of various kinds followed the same basic structure, and the shape flying toward them at high speed bore a strong resemblance to their own town. In fact, it was almost identical. The familiar rows of dwellings, the navigational control tower, and three-dimensional radar arrays all stood out in the sunlight. Perhaps the only point where the two towns differed was that all of the structures on the other town were reinforced with menacing armor plating. One look at the new town and its aim was apparent. The vessel was built to plunder.

Posing as an ordinary city, they might close in on their victims under a pretext of trade, then use their cannons to rob their prey of their defenses before sending armed troops to board. In other words, they were pirates of the sky. But, strangely enough, not only wasn't there a single person to be seen on the streets or in any of the ship's portholes, but no one was visible through the control room's window, either.

"That's odd—if this ship's here to loot us, they should be softening us up with their guns now," D heard the winded Dr. Tsurugi say from behind him. "But they're pulling alongside us instead. We'll have to fight them."

"What about the sheriff?" D asked, eying the pirate ship slowly circling them.

"He'll be here soon, I'm sure," the physician replied. "The real question is whether he'll be of any use or not."

"Why's that?"

"As you may already know, due to their overprotected state, people around here are incredibly susceptible to shock. The townsfolk here have had peace for too long. Fights and other disputes have always been the sort of things they could settle among themselves in their little town. Forget the fact they wouldn't know how to begin to deal with attackers from outside—the whole incident with the lightning has left the lot of them in a stupor."

"Then it's up to just the three of us."

A perplexed expression wafted over Dr. Tsurugi's face. "The three of us?" he muttered, paling instantly. "I can't believe you! You intend to have Lori fight? Why, she's just—"

"She has to live on her own." D's words had an edge like the wind.

After a bit of hemming and hawing, Dr. Tsurugi nodded. "You're right. That's what life on the Frontier is all about. But what'll we do?"

A sharp impact shook the ground they stood on. The enemy ship had finally pulled alongside the town.

D produced a memo pad from one of his coat's inner pockets. It was the same pad that'd been left out for Lori at the hospital. Eyes wide with astonishment, the physician wondered why he'd been carrying it around. Putting the tip of his forefinger in his mouth and nicking it open, D drew it across the memo pad. *Fight or die*, he wrote. *We want you with us.*

Us. That meant the three of them were going to fight together. Lori nodded fervently.

"But, what'll you have her do? She's an injured girl."

"Go to the weapons bunker and get us some arms. She'll carry the ammo and be in charge of reloading."

"Okay."

The two of them dashed away. D looked back at the blocks of buildings. As his companions' footsteps faded out, more rough footfalls arose to take their place. It was the mayor, the sheriff, and some of his men—four men in all. And the physician had said he didn't know if they'd be of any use . . .

There was another impact against their protective walls. From the deck of the pirate ship, several steel sheets extended toward the town. Hooks sank noisily into the top of the town's walls, and the sheriff and his companions unconsciously backed away. Every face was taut with fear. These men lived in a closed society where everyone understood just how tough they were supposed to be, but now that they faced invaders who wouldn't know the reputations they'd long relied on, they were reduced to cowards.

D's eyes narrowed ever so slightly. He waited, but what he waited for never appeared. Silence. . . Nothing happened.

While the planks had been laid for plundering, not a single blood-crazed outlaw appeared.

"What the hell is this, then?" one of the lawmen said, sounding rather relieved. "Are they just fucking with us or what? Not one of them has shown himself."

"They'll come out any second," another one said, his voice on the verge of tears. "And when they do, they'll rip us to shreds with some god-awful weapons. Damn it! God damn it all! Why do we gotta go up against these damn freaks?!"

The sheriff roared, "Knock it off! You're turning my belly. We're here now, so there's no use bitching about it. We ain't letting a single one of them marauding motherhumpers into town."

Compared to his compatriots, Hutton was certainly brave. In the wake of that outburst, his cowardly deputies readied their shotguns again. And yet, still—nothing happened.

The mayor looked at D suspiciously. "Somehow, I don't think they're toying with us . . ."

No reply came from the Hunter, but his black coat zipped past the men's noses. D stood on the gangway bridging the two vessels. Black hair streaming in the wind, coat fluttering, he trained his gelid stare on the deck of the enemy ship. Suddenly, he advanced without making a sound.

The men looked at each other. They must've realized protecting the town was an unavoidable part of their duty, but the mayor stayed where he was, led by the sheriff, while the others struggled up the wall and began to cross the same gangway. Just as they finished crossing the ten-foot-long plank, two things made the men grow pale—a strange aura and a stench. The aura could only mean death. And the stench was that of death as well.

Just moments earlier this ominous vessel had them fearing for their very lives, but now the unsettling silence did even more to start these rough men shaking. There was no sign of D. The men hopped down onto the street. Right in front of them lay the residential sector. The layout itself wasn't all that different from their own town.

"Pete, you and Yan find the control room. I'm gonna check out this area."

"But, Sheriff—this place gives me the creeps . . . "

"You damn fool! The way things are going, there's probably nobody on this tub. Maybe they took to killing each other, or some kinda epidemic broke out, but for all we know everyone could be dead. Now think for a second what that'd mean."

Pete's face, sullen until now, suddenly shone. "Oh, I get you! This here was a marauder ship. Meaning there's probably a load of treasure here."

"Damn straight! We'll tell the ol' mayor the town could use some of their energy surplus or their navigational computer or something, but the most precious cargo we'll keep for ourselves."

"Damn, you're a shrewd one. No wonder you're sheriff. But what'll we do about the Hunter that went on ahead of us?"

"That's pretty obvious. Kill 'im," said the other man, Yan, but he didn't know what D was capable of. While he knew about how D had killed the two deputies, not having seen it with his own eyes meant he found the account impossible to believe. "Lucky for us, the bastard's all caught up in searching the ship. It's a perfect chance to blindside him. What the hell—we can always say some automated defenses got him."

"That's real good thinking," the sheriff responded, but his words sounded hollow. He knew, as only someone who'd had the tip of D's blade pressed against their throat could, what a dhampir was capable of. "But don't lay a hand on him, you follow me? We'll just take whatever we want. I know how tough he is. You lump him in with normal Hunters, and you'll be in for a world of hurt."

"Yeah, but—" Yan began.

"We'll come up with some way to get rid of him later. You savvy? No matter what happens, you don't lay a hand on him," the sheriff said sternly, adjusting his grip on the rocket launcher.

Parting company with Pete and Yan, the sheriff walked into the residential sector. Unconsciously, he sought a sound or anything else that would show some sign of life. Anything would do. Some hint of murderous intent rising from malicious thugs in hiding. The snarls of vicious beasts just waiting to cross the gangways with their masters and sink their fangs into the windpipes of helpless victims. The sound of a safety being disengaged on an automatic crossbow. Anything at all . . .

But there was nothing except the . . . howling of the wind. There was no sign of anyone on the roads, where the artificial sand had blown away, leaving the underlying dirt exposed. There were just lines of dead trees down either side of the street, their branches rattling dryly. Dust catching in his throat, the sheriff pressed a handkerchief to his mouth. His cough created an unsettling echo in the otherwise still air. The sheriff shuddered.

The sky was blue. His own shadow stretched long and wide across the ground. And yet, the giant was nearly paralyzed with fear. Here was a town. It had buildings. It shot missiles. It pulled alongside them, then laid gangways for boarding. And yet, there wasn't a single crewman. How terrifying was that?

As Hutton was about to set off to look for the home of the local mayor—or, rather, the commander of this pirate ship—the tip of his boot struck something hard. When his eyes casually dropped to the ground, they ended up bulging from their sockets. It was a single bare bone. Most likely it'd been there for quite some time, as it was dried out and had a thin brown patina to it. It was clearly a femur. Seeing the severed end of it, the sheriff's eyes went wider still. It was burnt. There were signs of carbonization. As he rubbed it with his finger, some of it fell away as powder. This hadn't been charred little by little at a low temperature, as would happen in a fire. It'd been exposed to a blast of ultrahigh heat. Probably a laser.

For the first time, the sheriff noticed the white things haphazardly scattered about the place. There was a skull. And a rib cage. And another denuded skull resting on a pile of rags. As his eyes squarely met the skull's empty sockets, cold sweat started soaking his broad back. Stirring his mind to keep it from freezing solid with fear, the sheriff headed over to a shack that appeared to be a bar and the intact skeleton lying in front of it. The steel arrow jutting from its forehead was a vivid testament to the tragedy that'd unfolded here. One of the skeleton's arms was outstretched, and tight in its bony grip was a gleaming black automatic handgun of vintage design. Prying the weapon from its fingers, he examined it. All the ammo had been expended—most likely the result of a long, deadly conflict. But what in the world could've caused the roughneck crew of a pirate ship to start killing each other?

Sensing something behind him, the sheriff turned his gigantic form with lightning speed. Standing stock-still in the face of the seven barrels of his missile launcher were Dr. Tsurugi and Lori. "Oh, it's just you two . . . " he sighed. Wiping the sweat from his brow, the sheriff lowered his weapon.

"What in blazes is going on with this ship? What happened here?" Even the voice of the hot-blooded physician trembled a bit.

Looking around at their ominous surroundings and the remains at their feet, Lori seemed anxious, too. However, unlike the physician or the sheriff, she was completely detached from the whole world of sound, and this actually served to mitigate the terror for her to some degree. She and Dr. Tsurugi each carried a shotgun.

"Just what you see. Looks to me like they just went off on a goddamn killing spree. From the shape of these bones, I'd wager it was quite some time ago. And it looks to me like not one of them made it out alive."

"Well, they launched missiles at us. And put down gangways. Is that the sort of thing a crewless ship does automatically? For starters, we don't even know why they fired the missiles. They might've been small scale, but they were still nukes. If they'd scored a hit, they'd have most likely knocked the town out of the sky with one shot."

"So, failing to shoot us down, they decided to close with us," the sheriff spat. He looked at the skeletal faces, and, an instant after relief swept over him, the urge to plunder filled his head.

The presence of the doctor and Lori quickly became a hindrance to his plan. *They'll get theirs, too*, the lawman thought, a kind of madness suddenly at work in his mind. The barrel of the rocket launcher rose smoothly.

And that was when it happened. Screams echoed off in the distance. Two of them—Yan's and Pete's. Exchanging glances, the physician and sheriff started running as fast as they could toward the sound. The sheriff halted in front of the control center, where the iron door had fallen into the room. There was a blue tinge to the air, and the foul smell of burnt flesh hit his nose. Smoke was creeping out through the doorway. Someone was in there. *Don't tell me they went after D*, he thought.

Apparently realizing his duty as a lawman, the sheriff told Dr. Tsurugi, "You two stay right here." And then he slipped through the doorway alone. It didn't take long at all. At some point someone or something had utterly destroyed the control room, and on the floor lay a pair of charred corpses, one on top of the other. He didn't even have to look at them to know they were Pete and Yan's remains. An optical weapon with less output than a laser had burnt them to a crisp. Most likely it was a heat ray.

Shifting the rocket launcher to his left hand, the sheriff drew a huge explosive-firing handgun with his right. While its design closely resembled that of an old-fashioned revolver, it could hold thirty-six shots. The exploding rounds were powerful enough to drop a lesser dragon with one shot, or dispatch a medium-sized fire dragon with half a dozen. He couldn't very well start blasting away with his missiles indoors. Suddenly, a metallic sound reverberated from a pitch-black corner of the room. Looking over his shoulder, the instant Sheriff Hutton's eyes caught a semicircular shape, his handgun roared.

The deafening report of a weapon made Dr. Tsurugi tense up. Beyond the doorway, a red glow swelled momentarily, and an incredible shriek rang out. Lori clung to Dr. Tsurugi's arm, trembling. Though he'd told her to wait, the girl was determined to go with him. Apparently she could gather from the red light and Dr. Tsurugi's tension that something had happened. Slowly mouthing the words, "Wait here," Dr. Tsurugi pulled his arm free from her grasp.

Lori didn't disobey him. In her travels with her parents, she'd learned far too well what resulted when action was precipitated by curiosity or fear.

Laying both hands gently on the girl's shoulders, Dr. Tsurugi headed quickly for the doorway. His steps suddenly halted. With a strange sound, a dark figure appeared from the room. The doctor readied his shotgun. The first thing he saw was an arm-like protrusion that called to mind a thermal-ray cannon. Following that was the spherical body. And supporting that body from below were caterpillar treads like those of a tank.

"Get down!" the physician shouted as he shoved Lori out of the way, a wave of orange sailing right over him. The tremendous heat set the back of his white lab coat ablaze, and flames licked from his hair. Screaming, the physician writhed in pain. Cradling his head, he rolled his back against the ground in an effort to put out the fire.

Grabbing him by the scruff of the neck, Lori dove off to the side. A second heat shower narrowly missed the pair, striking the ground near where they lay. Without so much as looking at the physician's back, Lori shouldered the shotgun and pulled the trigger. The blast struck the dome-shaped torso, and the buckshot ricocheted off in all directions with a beautiful sound. Lori threw herself to the ground. There was no way to escape now.

The arm that was going to spray them with white-hot death, however, turned in the opposite direction along with the rest of its body. In the shadow of a building some fifteen feet away there suddenly stood a figure in black so beautiful and tragic it numbed even the electronic brain of this machine. Perhaps that was the reason why it was delayed a tenth of a second aligning the sights on its thermal-ray cannon.

Easily leaping over the shower of blistering heat his foe unleashed, D brought his longsword down, slicing the top of the machine's head into a half-moon shape.

Land of the Dead

CHAPTER 6

I

Sparks and electromagnetic waves shooting from the newly cut opening, the machine halted, and, in the very same instant, Lori threw herself on the physician. Rubbing against his body, she crushed out the still-smoldering fire. Giving off only bluish smoke now, Dr. Tsurugi moaned. Above her, the girl sensed someone moving. Lori looked up and moved her lips. *Hurry,* she mouthed. *We have to get him to the nurse quickly!*

"I should have a look at him first," D said slowly, and, helping Lori out of the way, he pulled off the physician's lab coat.

"I'm fine," the disheveled Dr. Tsurugi said as he tugged at his own hair. "It's not a serious burn. I can walk on my own. Kindly leave me be."

D stood up. Despite the other man's sharp tone, the Hunter didn't seem particularly angry. Without giving the physician another glance, he looked at Lori.

An awesome tempest of fear and self-loathing raged in the girl's eyes. *Didn't even try to help the doctor . . . I just . . . took the gun . . .*

"Well done," D said soberly. Of course, Lori had no idea how close to miraculous it was to hear those words coming from him. "If you hadn't taken that shot, the machine probably would've killed you both. You knew the doctor's burns weren't too bad."

But I . . .

"And when you took the shot, you even put yourself in front of the doctor," the Hunter continued. "Not many people would've done that."

The girl's eyes were gleaming. Only after D said those words did she realize just what she'd done.

"Yes, indeed," the physician said as his hand picked through the miserable remnants of his hair. "If you'd bothered with me, both of us would be checking into the hereafter. I owe you my life. Now, then—lead on. My nurse hasn't been any use since the magnetic storm. This time it'll be *my* turn to get looked at."

Lori nodded. The girl knew that she was needed now.

Just then, they noticed there was no sign of D. A few minutes later he reappeared from the door to the control room.

"What happened to the sheriff and his men?"

D simply shook his head.

"What the hell was that thing?" the physician muttered, his voice fraught with anger.

In reply, D merely said, "An internal defensive system for the ship, no doubt. It seems to be the only thing moving. The ship's crew died off three years ago."

"How do you know that?"

D pulled a yellowed ship's log from his coat. After the physician had run his eyes over the last page of it, ineffable shades of terror and misery colored his face . . . an expression that didn't fade for the longest time.

The crew of this pirate ship had grown weary of their aimless voyages. Though they freely sailed the skies, the floating cities and cargo-laden sailing vessels they preyed on were few and far between. What's more, when the pirate ship finally *did* get a chance to shine, all her opponents had either mounted heavy firepower or acquired three-dimensional radar and more powerful engines, making fight or flight the only viable solutions. The number of targets a pirate ship could go after had decidedly decreased. Apathy and ennui began to take over the ship, and before long many of the crew took their own lives, while the rest either started killing each other to stave off the boredom or grew sick and died. But the ion engines of the ship itself still ran, and could continue to do so until the end of time. Carrying nothing save a load of corpses, she continued her voyage across the boundless seas of fear.

"And the person who kept this log?"

"He was in his cabin," D said, "shot through the forehead."

"In that case, who in the world fired those missiles?"

"The computer must've been programmed to do that. Someone told it to go right on plundering even after they were all dead."

The physician shook his head in disgust. Looking at D, he asked, "And none of this bothers you? There's carnage all around us, and your expression says you don't feel a thing. What does it take to break that pretty face of yours? What could make you cry? Or make you laugh?"

"I've seen too much," D said dispassionately.

"Still—" the physician began to say, but then a mysterious light filled his eyes. "Okay, I understand about the missiles. But what about the gangways being sent over after they pulled alongside us? You mean to say that was programmed into their computers as well?"

"I don't know."

"I see. But . . . "

"Let's go."

D turned around. As the physician was about to ask him to wait, he heard a low groan beneath his feet. The ship was starting to move. "What in the name of—"

"It's setting off on another journey. A new voyage of plunder." D's voice trailed off into the distance.

The other two went after him. The whole ship was mired in an eeriness that staggered the imagination. Just as the three of them finished crossing the gangway, the pirate ship gradually began pulling away from the town.

"Where do you suppose she'll go?" asked Dr. Tsurugi.

Lori gazed at D. The same question swam in her innocent eyes.

Both of them had already noticed something—the dark destiny that hung over the pirate ship. Somewhere on it, something still survived: the will of the crew that'd grown tired, killed their compatriots out of that boredom, and ultimately programmed their computer with orders for indiscriminate destruction and marauding before they themselves disappeared. The ship would leave on another voyage. Without a destination, she was steered by a shapeless hand on a horrifying journey of nothing but murder and plunder.

D and his companions watched the ship's dwindling form for what seemed like ages.

"Mayor's not around, is he?" D said.

"Probably at home. It's kind of strange, though. Barring extraordinary circumstances, he's not really the type to sit on the sidelines in a situation like this . . . "

"You should send Lori back to the hospital. And don't forget to take those weapons. You should go back with her."

The physician scanned the area, a shaken look in his eyes. If a man who didn't run without good reason had turned tail, there could be only one explanation—something big had happened. Taking Lori by the hand as the girl wondered what was going on, Dr. Tsurugi walked off toward the hospital.

D headed straight for the mayor's house. Ming's daughter came out and told the Hunter her father was in the control room. Not even acknowledging the thick, syrupy gaze the young lady kept trained on him, D turned right around.

As the town slid into a calm afternoon, an unnatural atmosphere hung over everything. D alone understood. Only he saw the resemblance between the mood in town and the eerie atmosphere that hung over the pirate vessel.

As he slipped in through the control room door, a shadowy form blocked his field of view. Using just his left hand, D caught the man flying toward him like a rag doll. It was one of the men who worked in the control room. His lower jaw had been completely torn off, and bloodstains covered his chest like an apron. His eyes had rolled up in his head. Fear and massive shock had stopped his heart. It was the work of a monster, something beyond the human ken.

Gently setting the dead man down, D turned his gaze forward to the perpetrator. Weapon in hand, the mayor was frozen in place. In front of him stood another worker. Several corpses lay at the worker's feet. All of them had bulging eyes, and skin as pale as paraffin. There was no need to see the wound at the base of each neck.

The worker turned toward the Hunter. He was in his forties. According to the list the mayor had given D, his name was Gertz Diason.

"Careful, D! He's a vampire!" the mayor shouted.

The worker opened his mouth, displaying a pair of stark white fangs. Discarding the bloody lower jaw he had in his hand, he slowly walked toward D. He knew who the real foe was. His feet stopped moving. If the vampire knew who his enemy was, he also knew the extent of his enemy's power. Fear left a clear taint on his cruel face.

"When did he start acting strangely?" D asked. His tone was so tranquil in the face of this fearsome opponent that it absolutely beggared belief.

"Been like that ever since he got back a little while ago," the mayor replied. He was also rather composed. And not just because D was there. "About three hours ago, they let him go home for a nap. After he came back to the control room, it seems he attacked the nearest guy. When a second man went down, one of the workers came and got me."

"Where's the town going?" D asked, his question on an entirely different track.

The enemy snarled. Whipping up the air, he attacked D. It was an ill-conceived attempt. As he passed D's shadowy form, it became clear that the Hunter had his longsword in hand. The blade sank deep into the fiend's chest, and, as the menace dropped, the mayor let his shoulders fall.

"Is this the result of the Knights' experiments?" D asked softly. "Is this what you wanted to get your hands on? Is this the peace you idealized?"

"Stop it!" the mayor shouted. "The Knights succeeded in their experiments, I tell you. Right in that very house. I knew that much. What they produced was perfect. That's why I wanted their method! Because my own efforts turned out imperfect."

"You kept what you'd created alive, and hid it somewhere. Kept the failure your experiments had created, when the Knights had been successful."

A frightening silence descended. It was D who formed the silence, and D who broke it.

"What did you hope to accomplish by turning the people in your town into vampires? Did you want to make eternal travelers?"

The mayor's Adam's apple bobbed wildly.

II

Before they had made their way back to the hospital, Lori noticed that a ghastly atmosphere had shrouded the town. Someone was watching them, she felt, through the keyhole in a closed door, or through a crack in drawn blinds, or from a back alley entrance. Lori was going to latch onto Dr. Tsurugi's arm, but then thought better of it. He was the one who was really hurt here. This wasn't a matter of who was a man and who was a woman. Maybe she couldn't hear or speak, but the strong still had to take care of the weak. And neither strength nor weakness had anything to do with one's physical condition.

However, the road carried them back to the hospital without incident. Though the physician called out the nurse's name, there was no answer. "Looks like she's gone," he clucked. Then, flopping down into a rickety chair, he quickly grabbed a memo pad and handed it to Lori. *Stay in the hospital. You mustn't go outside. And don't forget that shotgun.*

Lori wrote a reply: *Okay, but you need to be taken care of first. Where's the medicine?*

Stored with the other drugs in the next room. You'll have to apply it to me.

Nodding, Lori straightened herself up. Her body brimmed with vitality. This was the joy of accomplishment. Leaning her shotgun against the wall, she hurried out of the examination room.

For a hospital that seemed so cramped, the drug storeroom alone was huge. This room held the keys to life for the whole town. Lori knew the name of the medicine she needed—after all, she was the daughter of two chemists. The various medicines were organized according to their usage. The jars she was looking for were stored next to the artificial-skin patches back on the farthest rack, stacked one shelf below the acid. Grabbing two jars and a heap of skin patches, Lori turned.

A woman in white was standing in front of her. It was the nurse. Her eyes were strangely red. Like she was angry.

I'm sorry, Lori mouthed slowly. As a nurse, the other woman would be used to things like that.

The woman's lips slowly twisted and formed a smile. From the corners of it, fangs peeked out.

Lori froze in her tracks.

The nurse's thick fingers latched onto the girl's frail shoulders. Lips that loosed the winds of hell slowly climbed up her throat.

Help me! Lori shouted. But no voice came from her. Of course it wouldn't. Though the girl struggled with all her might, the vampire's hands didn't budge. *Help me!* Lori screamed, not giving up. *Help! Please! Somebody, help me!*

They were cries no one could hear. The voice of despair, frail and futile. Lori knew at last she was truly alienated. Left in a world where she sought aid, but no one would come. She was its sole resident.

The significance of the sunrise she'd watched with D was swept away with everything else. Fear of the unknown filled the girl's mind.

When the nurse pressed her lips against the nape of Lori's neck, the girl reached out with her left hand and grabbed a jar on the shelf above. She smacked it against the woman's face with all of her might, and the jar shattered. White smoke enveloped the fiend's hateful visage. The nurse reeled backward. Acid had gone into her eyes.

Knocking the nurse out of the way, Lori ran. A hand as cold as ice caught her ankle. The chill spread throughout her body, and Lori grew stiff. There was a strong tug on her leg. Pulling her back to the fallen fiend. Another pull. Her body slid across the floor. Something heavy clambered onto her back, and Lori tried to give a scream.

No one came. The doors were closed. Something as minor as the sound of a glass jar breaking wouldn't reach the examination room.

Lori was mired in despair. Then, the pressure of someone sitting on her back suddenly vanished. Something black was oozing through the middle of the door. As the blackness took human shape, Lori looked up at it with teary eyes.

How have you been? a cheerful voice said in her head. Today it sounded terribly bold.

You can understand me, right? You understand what I'm saying, Lori thought back. *Please, you've got to help me!*

Just leave it to me, the voice agreed readily.

The nurse pulled herself up. She burned with a demonic urge to fight this new foe. As she held her hands out in front of her chest, the fingers were spread for clawing. Like an animal the nurse pounced, but the black shadow went right through her. A black semicircle jutted from the white chest of her uniform. The nurse collapsed in a heap.

In no time, the semicircle had vanished. Lori couldn't begin to imagine what kind of physical properties the weapon must've possessed.

How about that? That's what happens when a monster or two crosses my path. You wanna learn how to do this stuff, too?

I do, Lori thought, wishing it with all her heart. Telepathy—a way to speak without using words. A flying disk that could kill a servant of the bloodsucking Nobility with one blow. Lori had to have these things.

Then we should be able to do something here. I need to ask one favor of you, if that's okay.

Just name it. I'll do whatever you want.

Lori's feverish, trembling thoughts were overlaid with a man's cold laughter. *Well, it's like this . . .*

✝

A special kind of death was racing around town. Just now, it'd paid a visit to one house, and, after meeting it for just a few seconds' time, all five members of the family thudded to the floor. It couldn't drink their blood, and this displeased it. But it was fated not to drink the blood of its peers. You might say it was performing the same role as a kind of infectious germ.

Emanating from every inch of it were what could be called vampire bacteria. The bacteria entered into the unlucky people through their skin and then moved into their muscle cells, going all the way to the marrow of their bones. And then something else was born. Night's baleful energy sprang from the marrow of their bones, and their muscles grew ten times stronger. No matter how much damage the skin cells might take, they'd regenerate in a few seconds. Surpassing humanity in every respect, and terrifying them in every respect as well. All because of their lust for blood . . .

Less than five minutes after their visitor had left, the family members awoke. They felt the hunger. And there was another powerful urge as well. They had to make more of their kind. They'd been made to avoid competing with each other.

More of our kind—

Make more of our kind—

And then the family left their home behind, each member off to separately fulfill their common duty.

†

When D came to the hospital looking for Lori, he heard from a deathly pale Dr. Tsurugi how the girl had been attacked by the vampire nurse. The Hunter seemed to have only the slightest interest in the incident. "Was she okay?" he asked.

"More or less," Dr. Tsurugi replied.

And that was the end of it.

Gripping a memo pad and electromagnetic pen in her delicate hands, Lori wrote, *What can I do for you?*

D's well-formed lips began to move. "I want you to go to your old house."

Why?

"Your parents hid certain chemical and mathematical formulas somewhere in the house before they ran off. If we don't dispose of them once and for all, there's likely to be more trouble, and you've seen the abominable results of such experiments with your own eyes."

But I don't know anything!

"Was there any place in particular in the house where your parents often brought you?"

Yes, there was.

"That's what I need to know, and that's why you have to go with me."

Okay. Putting the pen down, Lori got up.

†

About the town—where do you think it's headed? Lori asked D as they walked along. Her lips merely shaped the words. She got no answer. Perhaps that was because it didn't matter.

Suddenly, D said, "Apparently a new destination's been programmed into the computers. That's where we're headed."

But where is that?

"Given our present course, a place where there's ruins and graves that belonged to the Nobility."

Why would we go to such a place?

"We'd have to ask whoever input the heading. Though I have a feeling I might know."

What do you mean by that?

This time D didn't answer her. The two of them entered the old Knight house.

"Now, then, if you could show me the place you mentioned," D said softly.

Lori nodded.

Not surprisingly, the first place they went was the laboratory, someplace that'd been searched thoroughly by both D and the black shadow.

My father was always tapping the top of that desk with his finger. He may have been hiding something.

D reached for the pressure-resistant desk crafted of mahogany. "Where did he hit it?"

Lori pointed at a certain section. Though the surface of the desk seemed perfectly normal, on closer inspection it appeared that just that one spot was a bit more faded than the rest.

D stroked the surface. "How about it?" he asked.

Although Lori couldn't hear what he'd said, her eyes were riveted to him. There was definitely something rising grotesquely from the palm of his left hand. It resembled a human face. Lori watched silently as its lips moved.

"Hmm. The surface has been finished with something to bring out the shine. But it's oddly light in the part she just pointed out. The problem doesn't seem to be the thickness of the coat, but rather the composition."

"Is the composition the same?"

"Nope."

"Okay. Stand back, please."

Lori backed away, just as she was told. After all, there was something she *had to do* to the young man.

D's longsword flashed out. The swipe of his steel was faster than any eye could follow. Cleanly sliced from the desk, the piece of wood in question landed in D's left hand. "Analyze it," D commanded.

"Damn, you're a regular slave driver," the mouth in his hand remarked with discontent.

D pressed the thin board into the palm of his hand. A second passed, then two, then three.

"Good enough," a cramped voice said, trickling out between the hand and the board.

D opened his hand. The face on his palm had been reduced to just a pair of lips. A red tongue hung from them. Apparently his left hand had analyzed the material by licking it, as evidenced by the fact the surface of the board was wet.

"The atomic arrangement of each element forms a single letter or digit in the formula. That's a real good hiding place. If any given element is too thick or too thin, the letter disappears."

"Yes, it certainly is clever. So—" D began to say, but, as he looked over his shoulder, a pale little hand slammed a wooden wedge into his chest. Staggering back, D thudded to the floor. Surely he never dreamed Lori would reach around from behind him to put a stake in him.

But, in fact, Lori hadn't driven a stake into him at all.

With the realization that D's body wasn't moving in the slightest, the girl's sweet countenance suddenly crumbled, and an indescribably crude smile surfaced in its place. The voice that came from her was that of a man. "Now that's the way you do it! That's one obstacle out of the way, I guess. I bet it never occurred to him I might slip into the little lady he trusted the most. No hard feelings, bucko. Everything in life just boils down to business."

When the girl smiled broadly once again, her expression was unmistakably that of John M. Brasselli Pluto VIII.

†

The town kept moving. D still lay on the floor with a stake through his heart. The mayor had come and was engaged in an uncharacteristically enthusiastic conversation with Lori, and somewhere in town Pluto VIII's body wasn't breathing at all, while his heart alone kept beating. Dr. Tsurugi knew none of this, but mantled as he was in a vague fear, he could do nothing but arm himself with a scalpel and a shotgun.

†

Those scattering the vampire plague were paying quiet calls on the houses in town, while those who had fallen waited impatiently for the sun to go down. And those intently watching the three-dimensional radar in the navigational control room discovered a vast expanse of ruins on the plateau some twenty miles ahead of them—and they were terribly shocked to find there was less than an eight-inch difference between the height of the plateau and their present altitude.

†

Okay, time to come up with a final price. How much are you offering, fancy pants?" Lori asked, her lovely lips twisting into a sneer. Needless to say, the falsetto voice belonged to Pluto VIII. "I've got the chemical formula and mathematical equations you need to become a Noble. You've gotta be willing to pay handsomely for that."

"Fine. Fifty million dalas."

"Don't make me laugh. We're not talking about a kid looking for his allowance here. With this, you'll be able to make people who can go about their lives just as they do now and only have to drink blood once or twice a month—you follow me? Naturally, they'd be able to walk in the light of day. They could fall into water without drowning. And they wouldn't need to eat. You could blast 'em with a rifle or laser or whatever and the damage still wouldn't kill 'em. Plus, their personality won't change at all. There's nothing but advantages to this, right? You don't go offering a lousy fifty million dalas for something like that."

"Make it five hundred million dalas, then," the mayor said, smiling broadly.

The offer had just grown tenfold, but Pluto VIII shook Lori's head from side to side. "Five hundred billion dalas—and not a bit less. After all, you're getting the secret to making supermen. And, as an added bonus, I already borrowed this little lady's body and got rid of the Vampire Hunter who was holding up the works. So you won't be getting any further discount from me. Hell, you want me to go tell everyone how you cut my throat wide open while I was in your maid's body? I hate to break it to you, but I can get into rotting corpses, too. I could work her vocal cords and have her testify if I had to."

After thinking a bit, the mayor nodded and said, "Okay. It's all for the good of my town. You'll get the price you named—five hundred billion dalas. But I'll need one thing to sweeten the deal."

"And what would that be?"

"In place of the Vampire Hunter you killed, I'll need you to take care of the last vampire plaguing us—he's one of my experiments gone wrong."

Pluto VIII said nothing.

"The man I let on board two hundred years ago gave me a certain chemical formula and a procedure for making humans into vampires. However, it proved too difficult for me to complete successfully. I had to wait two long centuries for a pair of geniuses like Mr. and Mrs. Knight to be born before my hopes could be realized. But then they ran out on me at the last minute. Didn't care for my orders that the fruits of their labor only be used on the residents of our town. They wanted to use it for the good of the whole world. The fools," Mayor Ming spat. "There's only a small handful of people who actually want to live in peace. Just try giving something like that to the world below. Before you knew it, they'd start murdering each other. Those who were going to live in peace would only wind up courting death. I conducted my own research without their assistance. Though two of my guinea pigs came extremely close to success, it was simply beyond my power to root out the vampire cruelty budding within them. And, unfortunately, both of them escaped. One of them targeted my daughter to exact his revenge, but he was destroyed by the Vampire Hunter. The other one is still active—spreading the vampire bacteria within him everywhere he goes."

"That's rich," Lori—or rather, Pluto VIII—said, clutching *her* belly as he laughed. "Sounds to me like the situation is proceeding just like you hoped it would. Care to tell me why you want the vamp killed?"

"The cruelty of the Nobility is so great, it drives even *them* mad. I'm sure you're aware not only of what their kind did to us, but also how vicious the disputes were that raged between fellow Nobles. I want the life of the Nobility. However, at the same time, that life must be one of eternal peace."

"You're a greedy cuss, I'll grant you."

"Say what you will. It would be difficult for me to say the present strain of Nobilitation would suffice, no matter what we might try. You'll have to hurry and dispose of him before he turns every last person in town into an imitation vampire. And if you don't like that, then the whole deal is off."

"Okay," Lori/Pluto VIII said, nodding. "I'll drop your freak with one shot. Consider it as good as done."

The intercom buzzed loudly.

"What is it now?" the mayor fairly barked.

"The town is approaching a plateau. Preparations for landing have already begun."

"Aha," Pluto VIII said, eyes gleaming. "Then I guess this must be the destination that got fed into your computers. It should be kinda fun to try and figure out why he'd do that."

"If he input these coordinates, it's pretty obvious that once we get there he'll gain some advantage. Hurry up and get rid of him."

"Understood." Nodding his agreement, Pluto VIII got up. "You said there's already been some victims, right? That's just too damn funny. Let's hope some of them at least *wanted* to be vampires . . . "

†

Leaving the mayor's home, Pluto VIII felt an unspeakably weird aura envelope his borrowed body. Twilight was approaching. The aura wasn't particularly concerned with him individually—it filled the very air. A vast number of sources for the unsettling emanations were moving about nearby.

"Well, I'll be damned. The ol' mayor sure took his sweet time moving on this, and now it looks like we're talking about more than half the town—this place is a freaking undead paradise," Pluto VIII muttered, walking down the street on Lori's beautiful legs.

A presence soon stirred in his vicinity.

"Came to play, did you?" Pluto VIII muttered, and Lori stopped in her tracks.

In the feeble darkness stood a motionless figure with black gloves on. The weird atmosphere seemed to radiate most strongly from his body.

"I've been waiting for you," Pluto VIII laughed. "I don't know where the hell you're taking this town or even why, but it's all over now. I'll make quick work of you, then get off this ride—once I get what I've got coming, of course. The know-how that made you immortal should fetch me a nice price elsewhere, too. It's too bad you won't get to see your buddies multiply, but you'll have to get over that."

Though it was unclear how exactly Pluto VIII manipulated Lori's supposedly nonfunctioning vocal chords, he had her talking a blue streak. He then made a broad wave of his right hand in his foe's direction.

The instant it looked like the flash of black was going to buzz through the foe's heart, the vampire sailed silently over Pluto VIII's head. With a speed that staggered the imagination, the vampire launched a kick.

Evading the blow with unbelievable agility for a man in a young lady's body, Pluto VIII hurled his disk-shaped weapon with a scooping motion. The weapon's aim was true, and it quickly ripped the vampire open from crotch to chest and showered the road with bright blood.

"Got 'im!" Pluto VIII shouted through the beautiful girl's face.

It was only a second later that same face froze solid. The darkness behind where the fiend had collapsed had just sent forth a tall youth of unearthly beauty.

"No, not you . . . " Pluto VIII groaned. "It can't be . . . I mean, even a dhampir . . . You couldn't just take a stake through the heart . . . "

"Too bad." D's soft voice ripped Pluto VIII's heart from his chest. "Tell me what you discussed with the mayor."

Pluto VIII backed away. Though he was looking for a chance to run, he realized that would be impossible.

"The girl's parents told you something, didn't they?" D said, but Pluto VIII couldn't even tremble at his softly spoken words. "Probably where they hid the procedure and formula they'd perfected for making humans into Nobility. Why would they leave something like that here in town when they ran off? Answer me that."

"Because they were ready to die." Perhaps Pluto VIII had reconciled himself to the notion of fighting D, because his voice was incredibly calm. "Think about it. They'd always had an easy life, safe and secure in their little town. What could they do out on the Frontier? Even if they had the tools for it, they still didn't have the heart. And Mr. and Mrs. Knight knew it. But what the two of them accomplished was just too big for them to throw away. Maybe they wanted to help the future generations or something, but I'm sure the better part of it was due to the lust for fame. And, after some consideration, they couldn't think of anyplace safer to hide it than this town. Is that a heartbreaking tale or what? Dying like dogs, forgotten out in some far corner of the Frontier after all they did . . . So, you know, I figured I might as well use what they found to earn myself a little coin . . . "

"Did you kill the Knights?"

"What do you mean . . . ?" Pluto VIII's eyebrows rose. He looked ablaze with indignation.

Ever serene, D continued, "I don't think it likely a pair of chemists would fail to notice their trailer's nuclear reactor was malfunctioning. They went outside and got eaten. Now, no matter how sheltered those scientists might've been, there's no way they wouldn't have known how dangerous it was to go outside on the Frontier in the dead of night. Unless, of course, you promised them they'd be safe."

"Hey, wait just a minute there!" Pluto VIII protested, sticking out his right hand to stop that train of thought. "Not to toot my own horn or anything, but I saved the little lady."

"Yes, because I was there. Molecular intangibility lets you go right through radiation. You couldn't bring yourself to let the dragons eat her, but figured you could kill her easily enough inside the vehicle—and that's where you made your mistake."

"You're unbelievable. You're just a walking heap of suspicion." A smile zipped across the pretty young face Pluto VIII was using. A wicked grin he hadn't shown before. "Though you're right about some of that stuff. You know, when I first met you I got a real bad feeling, and it looks like I was right on the money."

"What was the mayor's aim?" D said, as if he hadn't heard a word of Pluto VIII's chilling admission. "To turn all the townspeople into Nobility—into vampires?"

For a brief instant, D's longsword danced out and split the twilight with stark, white flashes. A pair of figures who'd been closing on him from behind silently fell to the ground.

With that momentary weakening of D's uncanny aura, Pluto VIII was swallowed by the darkness. "It's too late, D," he called back. "Too late. These folks have all been infected by the mayor's failed experiment. And now they're just gonna keep on multiplying. This town is finished. Well, it's just what the mayor hoped would happen. Trying to turn human beings into perfect Nobles is just flat-out impossible."

He was probably right. The visitor two centuries ago, the mayor, the Knights—each of them probably had a dream. The town rode on a dream, was in fact made of dreams. And now the town was waking from that dream. Waking with the worst possible results.

"I didn't wanna have to throw down with you," Pluto VIII said, "but there's no way around it now. Let's do it. I'll see you again in hell, fates willing!"

The instant D realized the baneful air directed at him was melting into the darkness, he shut both eyes. His longsword went into action. It had no problem at all slicing the disk blade into pieces that scattered through the air.

D charged. Around him, the wind roared.

There was nothing Lori/Pluto VIII could do. D's fist sank into the girl's delicate solar plexus, but it swept right through her body as if her body was mist. Once again, the superhuman ability known as molecular intangibility had come into play. Lori's body had been transformed into a runny, shifting shadow.

D turned around. Like a tuft of grass fluttering in the breeze, the shadow billowed down the street and faded into the ground without a sound. Not bothering to watch the black tip of its head disappear, D looked instead into the distance, at the vast expanse of sky and earth.

The route some mysterious hand had put the cursed town on carried them now over ruins that stretched as far as the eye

could see. Massive stone pillars, canopies, and streets stood naked and dejected in the lights shining from the belly of the flying town. Though it went without saying that all of these ancient constructs were cracked and crumbled and otherwise reduced to terrible rubble by the ravages of wind and time, for some reason this land had an even ghastlier atmosphere. Out on the Frontier, ruins that'd belonged to the Nobility weren't particularly rare. Nevertheless, this land didn't stir the deep feelings of loneliness usually associated with such sites. This place suggested only one thing—an unsettling evil. And D alone knew the form that evil would take.

From out of the shadows of meandering rows of stone pillars, shapes stirred as if they'd noticed the coming town—human shapes, moving as if enraged . . . or overjoyed.

"At last . . . we're here . . . " said a desperate sigh of a voice that made D turn. It was a dark, blood-spattered figure lying in the road a few yards away. Even after D saw that it was the same unnatural creature Pluto VIII's disk blade had bisected, his expression never changed.

"So, you were the one guiding the town?" He put the question to the corpse just as he would to any living person.

"That's right. Everyone in town has what it takes to become one . . . " he said, his voice weak, his breath ragged. By "one," he no doubt meant one of his kind. "This is where . . . all the failures meet. Not alive, but . . . unable to die. Cursed with an endless hunger, and a future without dreams . . . no place could be more fitting for the people of this town."

"Six more hours?" D muttered. That was how long it was until dawn. Such a short time for the tremendously long engagement that was about to begin.

"The failures number over five thousand . . . Will the living prevail, or will death sing its song of victory? No . . . It won't be either. That's what makes this the perfect fate." His final words mixing with laughter and a death rattle, the figure collapsed on the ground once more, never to move again.

Destruction echoed from somewhere in the distance. No doubt the vampirized townsfolk were attacking another house. Even if the law enforcement bureau had gone into action, with things this far along they wouldn't have been able to handle the situation. Besides, they'd probably already succumbed as well . . .

Glancing briefly down the road—in the direction of the hospital—D set off for the navigational control center. In no time at all he was there. About a dozen workers were thoroughly engrossed in inspecting their weapons. An extraordinary tension filled the room.

On seeing D, the mayor showed more relief than hostility. "I suppose I should thank you for coming," he said.

"Take a good look down there," D said softly. "This is the end of the road you started them on. Down there, five thousand things that couldn't become Nobility are waiting for five hundred living people. They think the residents of your town will make fitting companions."

"They were failures." The mayor looked tired. "But we were going to be a perfect new breed of humanity. A creature with the mind and heart of a human and the immortal flesh of a Noble, reveling in an eternal life free from the filth of the mortal world. I may have failed, but the Knights succeeded. And as soon as they did so, they tried to get out of town."

"The vampire who attacked your daughter was one you made, wasn't he?"

"That's right. I made two, and both of them escaped. One of them turned his fangs on my daughter, the other one is spreading his germs all over town now."

"Half the town's already been turned into vampires. If you want to hire me to do it, I'll take care of them." Despite the present situation, a Hunter was always a Hunter.

"Is this the end of everything, then?" The mayor put both fists to his forehead. And then, looking at D, he smiled with satisfaction. "No, not yet. So long as there are still decent folks in this town, my dream will never die."

Frigid light filled D's eyes. If one was mad for having a mad dream, then the mayor was already out of his mind.

Abruptly, the ground tilted forward. Some unsecured machinery crashed against the mayor's shoulder. No blood came from him, but blue lightning crackled out of the wound. He was a cyborg.

"Touchdown in seven seconds . . . " a technician clinging to a control panel exclaimed.

The town from the sky was descending to the earth it was never supposed to meet.

"Six seconds . . . "

In the ruins below, countless things were starting to stir.

They're here! They're here! More of our kind have come!

The grating sound of lids being pushed open on coffins of stone, wood, or steel, and the putrid stench. Pale hands protruded from the graves, and crimson eyes gazed out.

"Four seconds . . . "

As Lori headed for a dilapidated building, Dr. Tsurugi came running up behind her.

"Three seconds . . . "

The town was silent. As if no one had been there from the very start.

"Two seconds . . . "

A disk blade gleamed in Lori's right hand. It was actually a solidified chemical compound that would disappear once it'd served its purpose.

"Zero!"

Before the jolt threw the people into the air, the thunder of the impact shattered the windows of every house. Lori and the physician rolled across the ground. The shock wave became a heavy wind that blasted through the town, knocking houses at an angle and snapping off trees. Half of the townspeople were injured in some way or another. The other half were actually injured as well, but it didn't bother them.

"Engine nozzles have been damaged."

"We have cracking in the convection pipes."

Voices shot back and forth across the control room in confusion.

"How long will it take to input a new course and get airborne again?" the mayor asked.

"Four hours minimum."

"Do it in two."

"Roger."

D ran to the entrance. Warped by the impact, the iron door wouldn't budge an inch. D hit it with his shoulder. By the time the door hit the ground, sending scraps of metal flying everywhere, D's form was already racing down the darkened streets.

†

With silent footsteps, death's countless shapes were closing in on the town. Scrawny hands imbued with the strength to snap trees in two reached for the entrance hatch on the bottom of the town's base. The air outside began to stir with the dim sound of them pounding away at the door with their fists.

"They're getting in!" a bloodstained controller cried out.

"Relax. Even with the strength of a Noble, they couldn't break through that hatch," the mayor said as he smeared repairing compound on his shoulder wound. "We just have to hold out for two hours. Hook some power lines into the outer walls and the barrier. Juice them to a hundred thousand volts."

"Roger!"

Soon, the whole town was enveloped in pale light. The front rank of vampires reeled backward, smoking and giving off sparks. All of them had their hair standing on end.

"We did it!" one of the operators shouted.

"It's no use. The voltage is too high," another worker muttered.

One after another the shadowy figures emerged from the darkness. From behind stone columns and under domes. Out of the very ground. New bodies piled on top of the charred ones. Fire burst from the new ones, too. Planting their feet on the shoulders of the ones below them, they put their hands to the outer wall and began to scale it.

"They should be dead . . . but they're climbing up it," someone said.

And to that, someone else replied, "The Nobility are immortal . . . "

"Raise the voltage!" the mayor ordered. "We'll burn them down to the marrow of their bones. Deputies and security, head outside and shoot any intruders. We can't let a single one get on board."

The light had lost its bluish tint and was now stark white. The figures scaling the outer wall crumbled like clay figures cracked by the hot sun.

"They're running! We're saved!" someone shouted jubilantly at the sight of the retreating figures on the control room's screens.

"Don't let your guard down. They still have time yet. They'll be back again for sure. And we can't count on the barrier. Get outside and start shooting." As the relief of the present crossed the mayor's face, so did the fears of the future.

†

D was out in the middle of the street. The glow of the barrier had vanished, and, aside from the lingering stench, the town was peaceful and quiet. The people were now either locked in their homes cowering from this new threat or out seeking the blood of others. It seemed the latter had all became one with the darkness while spreading their death.

Figures appeared in front of D, and behind him as well. Crimson eyes filled with an atrocious hunger, they edged closer. It seemed that almost everyone in town had been turned into a fiend. There wasn't anyone left for him to protect now . . . aside from two people.

Something flew past the Hunter with the speed of a swallow. D knocked several more away with his left hand, and all the rest sank into the chests of the approaching figures.

Cries of pain split the darkness. The missiles were wooden wedges from stake-firing guns. The men from the law enforcement bureau didn't have time to fire a second volley, as people pounced on them from the roofs of various houses.

D's longsword flashed out, and several figures who'd been run through the chest fell to the ground. All of them were townspeople.

"Can't hold them off any longer. Prepare to abandon ship," D ordered the frightened, faltering lawmen as he lowered his bloody blade.

"We can't do that. There are tons of them outside. Wherever we go, they'll kill us. We'll just have to wait for daybreak," one of them said in a hollow voice. The only emotion coloring it was a deep shade of despair.

"Then do what you like." D turned and left without another word.

The town would rot away silently, as if this had all been decided two centuries earlier. For the town's people, tomorrow would never come.

As D hurried down the street, a pale figure rushed at him from the right side. Without even turning to look that way, D simply swept his right hand horizontally. When the figure fell with fresh blood gushing from its chest, D recognized the face. It was the little girl he'd saved from the colossal birds. The fangs jutting from her mouth slowly vanished.

†

D walked on. Before he got to the hospital, he was attacked several times, and each time was but a single exchange. Once he'd killed one, there was no one willing to make a second attack. The unearthly aura around D cowed even the dead.

D came to a halt in front of the hospital. The white building was completely destroyed. If the two of them were still inside, even a miracle wouldn't be enough to save them. Gazing at the rubble for a while, D turned.

A shadowy figure stood there like darkness congealed. Under either arm he carried a body. Dr. Tsurugi and Lori. "They're both okay, D," Pluto VIII said. "But I don't think you'll be able to get them safely out of here the way things stand now—plus, we've got us a fight to finish!" And, with the last word, he let the two bodies fall to the ground.

D sprang instantaneously.

Pluto VIII's body transformed into a black stain, and two disks flew from him. There was a silvery flash of light. The disks ricocheted away.

Shrinking and shifting, the black stain returned to the form of Pluto VIII. A dark line ran down his forehead. "Thanks," he said. "Noticed I didn't have much time left, did you?"

Bright blood spilled from Pluto VIII's mouth, but it wasn't the result of any wound D had dealt him. Just as he/Lori had been about to kill Dr. Tsurugi, the jolt of the town landing had dealt a grievous wound to Pluto VIII's real body wherever he'd left it sleeping.

"There's one thing I have to tell you . . . " Pluto VIII groaned as he slowly sank to his knees. "I took her body against her wishes. Tried swaying her with offers of telepathy—but she fought me to the very end."

"I know," D said, nodding. "But I'm sure she was always grateful to you for saving her, too."

It was unclear whether D actually caught the smile chiseled into Pluto VIII's face at the moment of death.

D went over to where the two bodies lay. They both had a pulse. More surprisingly, some of their cuts had been crudely bandaged. Pluto VIII must've done it. He was a strange man.

Screams rose in the distance. Residents were being attacked by former residents, by neighbors who finally had a goal, thanks to this need to turn everyone into vampires.

D put his right hand on the physician's brow. His eyes opened immediately. As his dim gaze bounced from left to right, there was a glint of will in his eyes. Staring at D, after a moment he asked, "Did you save us?"

"Not me. Him."

A sorrowful gaze fell on the lifeless form. "I just can't figure that . . . " the physician muttered. "What about the town?"

"This town died a long time ago. Now true death has come for it. But I'll get you both out of here safely. Rest assured."

"I give up . . . " Dr. Tsurugi said. "You're just too much for me. I finally see why *she* felt the way she did."

"What are you talking about?" D asked.

The physician said the name of a village, and D's expression changed. It was as if he'd just been touched by a gentle breeze in midsummer. Several years earlier, he was in that village, locked in a fierce battle to the death with a vampire to protect a brother and sister who lived on a ranch on the outskirts of the small town.

"Are they both well?"

The physician nodded. "Extremely. The little guy helps his sister out like a grown man, and their ranch is even bigger now. I would've loved to stay there doing what I could for the rest of my days, but it seemed she had her heart set on somebody else." Finishing his inspection of Lori, the physician nodded with satisfaction and straightened himself up.

"Where do you think you're going?" the Hunter asked.

"You don't know how to work the exits on your own, do you? Let me help you."

"You're wounded."

"I couldn't win that girl's heart. At least let me do something that would've made her happy."

D looked straight into the other man's eyes and saw the perplexing emotions that swam there. "How long did you spend in that village?" he asked.

"Not long. Six months."

"The two of them were lucky to have you."

"Thank you." The physician's eyes glittered. A look of pride shone in them.

†

"The barrier's voltage is dropping rapidly!"

As if in response to that last cry, shadowy figures that'd been headed away surged toward the town again.

"How goes inputting the course into the computers?" the mayor shouted.

"It's finished."

"Take her up then!"

"We don't have enough thrust, sir!"

"I don't care. Just do it!"

"Roger."

As pale figures cleared the outer wall, pouring down like an avalanche, the town escaped the bounds of earth. It bobbed up into the air as if that were its sole purpose. Still, a few shadowy figures came down the inner wall. The last thing they ever saw was a gorgeous young man who gave off the most unearthly air. Running every last intruder through the heart, D lowered his longsword and turned.

The mayor was standing there. "My journey has only just begun," he said. "As soon as the dawn comes, the vampires will be destroyed. I'm sure the remaining townsfolk and I will somehow manage to keep the town running."

"This is a dead town," D said quietly. "Where will you go? And for what purpose?"

The mayor laughed. It sounded ghastly. A figure leapt at him from behind, its fangs bared. The mayor's fingertips sank into its heart, and the figure fell at his feet. It was Laura.

Off in the distance, the wind howled. The dawn was still far off.

"There's a plain a dozen miles from here. You and your friends get off there." The very sound of the mayor's voice was dark and distant.

†

Saying not a word, the trio watched the departing town. Where would it go? No trace of the formula had been found on Pluto VIII's body . . . Where could he have hidden it? Would the mayor ever find it again?

D stroked the muzzle of his cyborg horse. It was one of three the mayor had left with them.

"What'll we do about the girl?" the physician said, believing Lori to still be asleep, but when he looked over his shoulder he found her awake.

Her eyes gazed across the plain at the blue dawn. Her pale finger moved across the sand. The two men read what she'd written. *I've heard the sound of the wind and the songs of the birds*, it said. So, that was the perspective the girl had after seeing life and death up close? As her long hair fluttered in the morning breeze, Lori's shadow was etched distinctly on the ground.

"A mile and a quarter ahead of us is a town. The two of you should go there together." Saying that, D got on his steed.

"Where will you go?"

Giving no reply, D advanced on his horse. Mount and rider quickly dwindled as they headed off, bound for the mountain ridges that grew bluer by the minute.

Postscript

T his is my first new postscript for the English editions of my books.

I'd like to thank my readers in America and elsewhere for supporting D for so long. Due, no doubt, to the two animated features, sales of the novels have been good, and the author is overjoyed. I can't sleep with my feet toward the anime directors. (According to Japanese custom, sleeping with your feet facing someone you are indebted to means you aren't grateful to them. Well, since I don't know where either of them lives, I may actually have my feet pointed toward them . . .)

I've loved horror and sci-fi since I was a kid, and I never missed one of these kinds of films when they were showing in my hometown (which was a desolate port town like Lovecraft's Innsmouth.) Even when I had a fever of about a hundred and four, I acted perfectly fine in front of my parents, and, once I was outside, I staggered over to the movie theater. (The film was *The Brides of Dracula*.) Hammer's *The Revenge of Frankenstein* was showing on the same bill with a rather erotic French film, and the woman at the ticket booth said to me, "For a kid, you've come to see a pretty lewd movie." But I pretended I didn't know what she was talking about and went right on in. Unfortunately, the erotic film proved more interesting. (Laughs.)

As I was born in 1949, what left the strongest impression on me were the Hammer horror films from England. In particular, I'll never forget the impact *Horror of Dracula* had on me when I saw it. Gripped by the fearsomeness of Count Dracula as portrayed by Christopher Lee, every night I slept with a cross fashioned from a pair of chopsticks by my pillow.

Mr. Lee and Peter Cushing, who played the part of Van Helsing, became my favorite stars. Though I never did get a chance to meet Mr. Cushing, about ten years ago I met Mr. Lee and got his autograph when he came to Japan for the Tokyo Fantastic Film Festival. Wow, was he huge! (I'm not quite five foot seven.)

But the first time I ever saw Dracula and Frankenstein, the Wolf Man, mad doctors, and the rest was in a horror/comedy production by Universal called *Abbott and Costello Meet Frankenstein*. Made in 1948, the film was screened in Japan in 1956.

All of the monsters who were to decide my future were in this one film. How lucky could you get? I think I was somehow fated to write about them. And the way I completely missed *Horror of Dracula* the first time it showed in my hometown but caught it when it came back for another showing a few years later was nothing short of miraculous. Once again, it was destiny.

This is how the hero known as Vampire Hunter D came to be. I was thirty-three when I gave life to him, and I continue writing about his adventures twenty-two years later. Not only in novels now, he's spread to animation and games, and plans for his Hollywood debut and an American comic version are progressing nicely. However, more than anything, it pleases me that the novels have found acceptance and an audience with you.

I'm quite proud of *Tale of the Dead Town* and the action I penned as D does battle with the Nobility against the wondrous backdrop of a floating city. Please sit back and enjoy it, just as you'd watch a scary, fun, and thrilling horror/action movie.

Until we meet again. From under distant Japanese skies, to all my readers abroad.

Hideyuki Kikuchi
October 14, 2005,
watching *Horror of Dracula*

And now, a preview of the next novel in the
Vampire Hunter D series

VAMPIRE HUNTER D
VOLUME 5
THE STUFF OF DREAMS

Written by
Hideyuki Kikuchi

Illustrations by
Yoshitaka Amano

English translation by
Kevin Leahy

Now Available
from Dark Horse Books and Digital Manga Publishing

The Girl the Sleep-bringer Loved

I

The moon was out.

No matter how dangerous night on the Frontier had become, the clarity of the night itself never changed. Perhaps supernatural beasts and fiends alone had pleasant dreams . . .

But there was someone else here who might have them, too. Here, in the middle of a dense forest, he slept.

As if to prove that night on the Frontier was never silent, voices beyond numbering sang from the tops of the demon's scruff oaks or from the dense greenery of a thicket of sweet mario bushes.

Though the sleeper's dreams might be peaceful, the forest at night was home to hunger and evil. Spraying poison to seal their opponent's eyes, dungeon beetles were known to set upon their prey with sharp teeth no bigger than grains of sand. A swarm of them could take a fifteen-foot-long armored dragon and strip it to the bone in less than two minutes. Sometimes the black earth swelled up, and a mass of absorption worms burst out, crawling in all directions. Over a foot and a half long, the massive worms broke down soil with powerful molecular vibrations and absorbed it through the million mouths that graced the nucleus of each of their cells. Usually they'd latch onto a traveler's ankle first and melt the foot right off before pouncing on more vital locations like the head or the heart. How could anything escape them when their very touch ate through skin and bone alike?

Colors occurred in the darkness as well. Perhaps catching some odd little noise in the sound of the wind, the snowy white petals that opened gorgeously in the moonlight trembled ever so slightly as the flower sprayed out a pale purple mist, and, as the cloud drifted down to earth, tiny white figures floated down with it. Each of them carried a minute spear, and only those who'd made it through the forest alive knew that they were evil little sprites from within the flower, with poison sap made from petals.

And of all the blood-hued eyes glittering off in the darkness a little way off, and further back, and even deeper still—nothing—was merely an innocent onlooker.

While everyone who went out on the Frontier might not know it, those who actually lived there realized the forests weren't a wise place to choose for a night of restful sleep. They were aware that the plaintive birdsong was actually the voice of a demon bird that muddled the senses, and that the gentle fog was in fact mist devils trying to sneak into their victims' bodies. If they absolutely had to sleep in the forest, people would keep a bow with an incendiary-tipped arrow in one hand, and shut their eyes only after zipping their asbestos sleeping bag up over their head. Sprite spears and the teeth of nocturnal insect predators couldn't penetrate a half-inch thickness of that cloth, and, if a traveler drank an antidote derived from the juice of hell berries, they didn't have to worry about demonic fogs, either. Their head, however, would be aching the next morning. If, by some chance, the attacks should persist, then the bow and arrow came into play.

However, the traveler now surrounded by all these weird creatures seemed completely ignorant of the threats the woods held. Lying on a bed of grass, the moonlight shone down on him like a spotlight. While his face couldn't be seen for the black, wide-brimmed traveler's hat that covered it, the deep blue pendant that hung at his chest, the black long coat, the high leather boots with their silver spurs, and, more than anything, the elegant longsword leaning against his shoulder left no room for muddled conjecture or doubt. All those things were meant to adorn someone beautiful.

However, part of his description was still lacking. Watch. When the monstrous creatures blanketing the ground come within three feet of the traveler, they rub their paws and pincers and begin to twitch uncontrollably, as if checked by some unseen barrier. They know. They understand. Though the traveler sleeps, something emanates from his body—a ghastly aura declaring that any who challenge him will die. The creatures of the wild know what the young man actually is, and the part of his description that is absolutely indispensable: He is not of this world.

The young man in black went right on sleeping, almost as if the poisonous mists of the sleeper grass smelled to him like the sweetest perfume, as if the indignant snarls of the ungodly creatures sounded to his ears like the most soothing melody.

Consciousness suddenly spread through his body. His left hand took hold of his hat, and, as he sat up, he placed it back on his long black hair. And anything that looked upon him realized that unearthly beauty did indeed exist.

People called him D. Though his eyes had been closed in sleep up until this very moment, there wasn't even a tiny hint of torpor in them. His black, bottomless pupils reflected another figure in black standing about ten feet ahead of him. Well over six and a half feet tall, the massive form was like a block of granite.

A certain power buffeted D's face, an aura emanating from that colossal figure. An ordinary human would've been so psychically damaged by it that they'd spend the better part of a lifetime trying to recover.

In his left hand, the man held a bow, while his right hand clutched a number of arrows. When bow and arrow met in front of that massive chest, D's right hand went for the handle of his longsword. The elegant movement befitted the young man.

An arrow whined through the air. D stayed just where he was, but a flash of silver rushed from his sheath and limned a gorgeous arc. When the smooth cut of his blade met the missile's beautiful flight in a shower of sparks, D knew his foe's arrows were forged entirely from steel.

The fierce light that resided in his opponent's eyes looked like a silent shout. The instant their respective weapons had met, his arrow was split down the middle, and the halves sank deep into the ground.

D stood up. A flash of black ran through his left shoulder. The black giant had unleashed this arrow at the same time as his second shot. Perfectly timed and fired on an equally precise course, the arrow had deceived D until it pierced his shoulder.

However, the black shadow seemed shaken, and it fell back without a sound. He alone understood how incredibly agile D had been, using his shoulder to stop an arrow that should've gone right through his heart.

As his foe backed away, D readied himself. Making no attempt to remove the arrow, he gazed at the giant's face with eyes that were suspiciously tranquil. D was reflected in his opponent's eyes as well.

"Don't intend to tell me your name, do you?" D's first words also held the first hint of emotion he'd shown. An instant later, the hem of his coat spread in midair. The blade he brought down like a silvery serpent's fang rent nothing but cloth as the black figure leapt back another fifteen feet. As his foe hovered in midair, the *twang* of a bowstring rang out. With as mellifluous a sound as was ever heard, the long, thin silhouette of the Hunter's blade sprang up, and D kicked off the ground with all of his might.

His foe was already partially obscured by a grove a hundred yards ahead. The few hundredths of a second it'd taken him to draw back for his third shot had proved critical.

Still not bothering with the arrow in his left shoulder, D sprinted into action. Inheriting much of the Nobility's powerful musculature in their legs, dhampirs could dash a hundred yards in less than six seconds. With his speed, D covered the distance in under five seconds, and he showed no signs of slowing. However, the shadow had been lost in the darkness. Did D sense that the presence had abruptly vanished?

He kept on running, and, when he halted, it was in precisely the same spot where his foe had disappeared. D had noticed that the deep footprints that'd led him that far ended in the soft grass.

His opponent had vanished into the heavens or sunk into the earth—neither of which was especially uncommon in this world.

D stood still. Black steel jutting from his left shoulder and fresh blood dripping from the wound, D hadn't let his expression change one bit throughout the battle. But the reason he didn't extract the arrow wasn't because he didn't feel the pain of it, but rather because he simply wasn't going to give his foe an opportunity to catch him off guard.

Frozen like a veritable statue, he broke his pose suddenly. Around him, everything was still and dark. The air of their deadly conflict must've stunned the supernatural creatures, because not a single peculiar growl or cry could be heard.

D's face turned, and his body began moving. There hadn't been any road there from the very start, just a bizarre progression of overlapping trees and bushes. Like an exquisite shadow, he moved ahead without hesitation, finding openings wherever he needed them. There was no telling if it would be a short hike or a long, hard trek. Night on the Frontier was a whole different world.

The wind bore a sound that was not its own whispers. Perhaps D had heard it even at the scene of the battle. Beyond the excited buzz of people and a light melody played by instruments of silver and gold, he could make out a faint glow.

The stately outline that towered protectively over the proceedings looked to be that of a chateau. As the Hunter walked closer, the outline gave way to rows of bright lights. Presently, D's way was barred by a gate in the huge iron fence before him. Not giving his surroundings a glance, D continued forward. Before his hands even touched it, the gate creaked open. Without a moment's delay, D stepped onto the property. Judging by the scale of the gate, this wasn't the main entrance.

Ahead of him was a stone verandah that gave off a shimmering light. The glow was not due to the light of the moon, but rather it radiated from the stones themselves. In the windows behind the verandah were countless human figures. Some laughed gaily. Some danced with elegance. The sharp swallowtails of men's formal attire flicked back and forth, and the hems of evening gowns swayed. The banquet at the mansion seemed to be at its height.

D's gaze fell to the steel jutting from his shoulder, and he took hold of it with his left hand. There was the sound of tearing flesh as he yanked the steel out, vermilion scraps of meat still clinging to it. As fresh blood gushed from the wound, D covered it with his left hand. It sounded like someone was drinking a glass of water. All the while D kept walking, climbing the stone steps of the verandah and then reaching for the doorknob. The bleeding from his shoulder hadn't stopped.

The doorknob was a blue jewel set in the middle of golden petals, and it turned readily in his well-formed hand.

D stood in a hall filled with blue light. One had to wonder if the young man realized that hue was not the white radiance he'd seen spilling from the windows. Perhaps the mansion was mocking D, because now only two figures danced in the room. The girl must've been around seventeen or eighteen. The fine shape of her limbs was every bit as glamorous as her dress, which seemed to be woven from obsidian thread, and each and every strand of the black hair that hung down to her waist glittered like a spun jewel. The light melody remained. Her partner in tails was also reflected in D's eyes. Still turned the other way, his face couldn't be seen.

D stepped further into the hall. It was clear the mansion had been meant to draw him there. If it had only two residents, one or both of them must've arranged this.

The girl stopped moving. The music ceased as well. As she stared at D, her eyes were filled with a mysterious gleam. "You're . . . ?" Her composed voice made the light flicker.

"I seem to have been invited here," D said as he looked at the back of the man who was still facing away from him. "By you? What's your business? Or where is he?"

"He?" The girl knit her thread-thin eyebrows.

"If you don't know who I'm referring to, perhaps that man does. Well?"

The man didn't move. Perhaps her partner was fashioned from bronze, and made solely to dance?

Asking nothing more, D plowed through the blue light to stand just behind the man. His left hand reached for the man's shoulder—and touched it. Slowly, the man turned around. Every detail of the girl's expression—which couldn't be neatly classified as either horror or delight—was etched into the corner of D's eye.

D opened his eyes. Blue light graced his surroundings. It was the pale glow of dawn, just before sunrise.

Slowly, D rose from his grassy resting place. Had it all been a dream? There was no wound to his left shoulder. Where he was now was the same spot where he'd gone to sleep. The cyborg horse that'd been absent from his dream stood by the tree trunk to which its reins were tied.

As the Hunter took the longsword and sheath in his left hand and slung it across his back, a hoarse and strangely earnest voice said, "No, sirree. That was too damn real for a plain old dream. Hell, it hurt *me*." The voice must've been referring to the steel arrow that'd penetrated the Hunter's left shoulder. "That mansion was calling you, sure enough. And if they called you, they must have business with you. Bet we'll be seeing them again real soon."

"You think so?" D said, speaking in the real world for the first time. "I saw him."

"Indeed," the voice agreed. But it sounded perplexed.

Setting the saddle he'd used for a pillow on his horse's back, D easily mounted his steed. The horse began walking in the blue light.

"How about that—it's the same!"

What the voice meant was this locale they'd never seen before bore a striking resemblance to the place in the dream, suggesting . . . that the source of the voice had the very same dream as D.

In a few minutes, the horse and rider arrived at an empty lot surrounded by a grove of sizable trees. This was where the mansion had been. A banquet in endless warm, blue light, light that spilled from the windows as men and women danced in formal wear, never seeing the dawn. Now, everything was hidden by the green leaves of vulgar spruces and the boughs of poison firs. Giving the landscape a disinterested glance, D wheeled his mount around. Beyond the forest, there should be a real village settled almost two hundred years ago.

Without looking back, the rider in black vanished into the depths of a grove riddled by the light of dawn, as if to say he'd already forgotten his dream.

II

D came to a halt in front of the gate to the village. Like any other village, it was surrounded by triple walls to keep out the Nobility and other foul creatures. The sight of verdigris-covered javelin-launchers and flamethrower nozzles poking out of those stockade fences was one to which most travelers would be accustomed. The same could be said for the trio of sturdy, well-armed men who appeared from the lookout hut next to the gate. The men signaled to D to stop. But one thing was different here— the expression these men wore. The looks of suspicion and distrust they usually trained on travelers had been replaced with a strange mix of confusion and fear . . . and a tinge of amity.

As one of them gazed somewhat embarrassedly at D on his horse, he asked, "You're a Hunter, ain't you? And not just any Hunter. You're a top-class Vampire Hunter. Isn't that right?"

"How did you know?" The soft sound of the man on horseback's voice cut through the three of them like a gust of wintry wind.

"Never mind," the man in the middle said, shaking his head and donning an ambiguous little smile as he turned back to the gate. Facing a hidden security camera, he raised his right hand. With the tortured squeal of gears and chains, the gate with its plank and iron covering swung inward.

"Get going. You're going in, right?" the first man asked.

Not saying a word, D put the heels of his boots to his horse's belly. As if blown out of the way by an unearthly wind gusting from the rider and his mount, the three men slipped off to either side, and D went into the village.

The wide main street ran straight from the gate into the village. To either side of it were rows of shops and homes. Again, this was a typical layout for a Frontier town. The kind of looks that'd greeted D outside the gate moments earlier met him again. People on the street stopped and focused stares of fear or confusion or affection on him, but it was the women whose gazes quickly turned to ones of rapture.

Ordinarily, women on the Frontier never let down their gruff and wary facade, even when the most handsome of men passed within inches of them. They were well aware that a pretty face didn't reflect the mind behind it. For all they knew, they might be the only one who saw him that way. What guarantee did they have that he wasn't, in fact, a poisonous crimson spider—a creature that not only had the power to hypnotize, but who could also give substance to hallucinations? Who could say for certain he hadn't been sent by bandits planning to burn the village to the ground and make off with all their money and their women? To crack the Frontier woman's hard-bitten demeanor took a beauty that was not of this world.

When he'd ridden halfway down the street—passing through odd looks and ecstatic gazes—a young woman's voice called out to his black-clad back, "Um, excuse me!" Her voice suited the morning.

D stopped. And he didn't move a muscle after that.

There was the sound of someone's short, quick steps on the raised wooden sidewalk off to D's left, a head of black hair slipped right by his side, and then the girl turned in front of him. A smile graced her face, which was fresh and rosy and bursting with youthfulness.

"You're a Vampire Hunter, aren't you?" The words were formed by lips painted a faint shade appropriate to her age. She was sixteen or seventeen—at the stage where she wanted people to look at her. Without waiting for an answer from D, she continued. "Well, if you are, please go out to the hospital on the edge of town. Sybille is in room seven."

D's expression shifted. Apparently, he'd recognized the girl, in her snowy white blouse and blue skirt with wine-red stripes, as someone worth talking to. "Have we met before?" he asked.

The girl's form tensed. D's tone was no different from what he'd used with the men out at the gate. It wouldn't be the least bit strange for it to leave a timid girl quaking. But this young lady just bobbed her head vigorously. "Yes. Only it—oh, just hurry!"

"Where did we meet?"

The girl smiled wryly. "You wouldn't believe me if I told you. It's better you hear it from someone upstanding, like a grown man, instead of from me. Hurry up and get to the hospital. The director will be so happy to see you."

It was a bizarre discussion. Although somewhat lacking in explanation, it was clear from the tone of the girl's voice that this was an urgent matter. What sort of conclusions were being drawn in the heart beneath that black raiment?

Asking nothing further, D resumed his advance. Once he was off the main street, the Frontier land rapidly grew more desolate. Almost all of the arable land had been bequeathed by the Nobility, given with the knowledge that fields which scarcely provided enough to survive were good insurance against insurrections. Of course, after the decline of the Nobility, there were some villages where crops and soil had been repeatedly improved, and, as a result of centuries of persistent toil, the townspeople had managed to make bountiful harvests a reality. But such successes never went any farther than the village level—they never spread across whole sectors. This desolate earth bore mute testimony to the fact there were only a dozen places on the entire Frontier that tasted such bounty, while elsewhere the battle against misery and poverty continued as it had for centuries.

But this community was actually one of those rare exceptions. As D's eyes ran along the edge of the village, he saw vast expanses of fragrant green forests and farmland, all of which seemed to be nestled between hills covered with neat orchards of verdant fruit trees. This village of five hundred harvested enough to feed nearly twenty times that number. Four times a year, when the entire village was done packing up their bounty, fifty massive transport vehicles hauled the town's excess food roughly sixty miles south to the freight station, where it was then shipped out to more impoverished villages on the Frontier or to the distant Capital. The reason homes and infrastructure in this village showed comparatively little wear was due to the income generated by their food surplus.

Following an asphalt-paved road for another five minutes, the Hunter saw a chalk-white structure atop a respectable-sized hill. The rather wide road forked off in several different directions before continuing up the slope. The flag that flew from the three-story building at the top of the hill had a five-pointed star on it—the mark of a hospital.

This must've been the place the girl had told him to go. But he'd never had any intention of doing what she asked . . .

The complete antithesis of the refreshing blue sky and greenery of morning, the black rider and horse reached the base of the hill at their own leisurely pace. Although the young rider didn't appear to pull back on the reins, his horse came to an immediate stop. Soon the beast changed direction, as if looking up at the hill, and they began to slowly ascend.

Twining the reins around a fence by the entrance, D went through the front door. The doors were all glass and were fully automated. As there probably wasn't a power station nearby, the doors must've run on the material fluid power that'd recently gained popularity. But the village would have to be incredibly well-off if they could afford to use that recent innovation on something so trivial.

D went over to the information desk beside the door. The nurse behind the desk had a mindless gaze and a vacant expression on her face. Of course, the same went for the female patients and other nurses dotting the vast lobby. This was beyond the level of just feverish stargazes—they seemed like their very souls had been sucked out.

"I'd like to see the person in charge," D told the nurse in a low voice.

Reaching for a switch under the desk, the woman said, "He'll be right here," though it was nearly a moan. Her syrupy tone seemed to have an almost wanton ring to it.

"He needn't do that. I'll go to him."

"No," the nurse said, shaking her head, "he expressly told me to let him know the moment you came in."

"So, he knows me, then?"

"Yes. Actually, so do I . . . "

It'd happened again.

D looked at the nurse. The light of reason had already left her eyes. He turned to the far end of the lobby.

Just then, footsteps echoed from one of the numerous corridors, and a figure in white came running toward him. The figure became an old man with a white beard who crossed the lobby at a lively pace and halted in front of the Hunter. Gazing steadfastly at D, he moaned, "Oh, my!" By the look on his face, he wished he were a woman. "Looks like I'll have to move my female patients and nurses somewhere else. I'm Allen, the hospital director."

"Call me D," the Hunter said in his usual brusque manner. "So, do you know me, too?"

Director Allen nodded deeply. "Though I only just met you *last night*. Looks so good it even made a man like me lightheaded—not a chance I'd forget that. So, what brings you here?"

"A few minutes ago, a girl told me to come here."

"A girl?" the aged director asked. His expression grew contemplative, and he asked, "Was she about sixteen or seventeen, with black hair way down to her waist? Pretty as no one's business?"

"Yes."

"That'd be Nan. Not surprising, really. You're just the man for the job."

"How did you know I'd come?"

"That was the impression I got last night." As he finished speaking, the hospital director swallowed hard. D was calmly gazing at him. The black of his eyes, impossibly dark and deep, awakened fearful memories etched in the very genes of the director's cells. Small talk and jokes had no place in the world of this young man—this being. Director Allen did all he could do to look away. Even when the young man's image was reduced to a reflection on the floor, the director was left with a fear as chill as winter in the core of his being.

"Please, come with me. This way." His tone bright for these last few words alone, Director Allen started retracing his earlier steps. Traveling down a number of white corridors, he led D to a sickroom. A vague air of secrecy hung over this part of the hospital. There wasn't a single sound. The room was surrounded by noise-dampening equipment that worked almost perfectly.

"So we don't wake the sleeping princess," the director explained as he opened the door, seeing that D had noticed the arrangements.

This place had turned its back on the light of day. In the feeble darkness of the spacious sickroom, the girl lay quietly in her bed. Her eyes were closed. Aside from the usual table, chairs, and cupboard, there wasn't any other furniture in the room. The windowpane behind the drawn curtains was opaque.

The dream last night, the watchmen at the gate, and the girl with the long hair—they all had to be part of a plan to lead D here. But toward what end?

The girl didn't seem to be breathing, but D stared down at her in pensive silence.

You should be out laughing in the sunshine.

"This is Sybille Schmitz—she's seventeen," the director said, hemming and hawing a bit when he came to her age.

"How many decades has she been like this?" D asked softly.

"Oh, so you could tell, then?" the hospital director said with admiration. The fact of the matter was she'd been that way for nearly thirty years. "One fall day, she was found lying out in the woods not far from the village. Right off we knew what'd been done to her. She had those two loathsome marks on the nape of her neck, after all. The whole village pitched in and we took turns watching her for three days without sleep so no one could get near her. In the end, the guilty party never did appear, but Sybille didn't wake up, either. She's been sleeping here in my hospital ever since. Our village was just about the only place that got along with the Nobility, so I don't see why something like this had to happen."

It was unclear if D was really listening to the man's weary voice. In this whole absurd business, D had confirmed only one thing as fact. A young lady dancing on and on with elegant steps in the blue light. People laughing merrily at a never-ending banquet. D turned to Director Allen. "How did you know I'd come?"

The hospital director had a look of resignation. "I had a dream about you last night," he replied more forcefully than necessary. He still hadn't fully escaped the mental doldrums the young man's gaze had put him in.

D didn't react at all.

"And not just me," Director Allen added. "Now, I didn't exactly go around checking or anything, but I'd wager the whole village did, too. Anyone who had that dream would understand."

"What kind of dream?"

"I don't remember anymore. But I knew you were going to come. You'd come to see Sybille."

Dreams again?

"Have there been any strange incidents in your village recently?"

The director shook his head. "Not only hasn't there been any problem with the Nobility, but we haven't had any crimes by outsiders or villagers, either. I imagine arguments and fisticuffs between those who've been hitting the bottle hardly qualify as the kind of incidents you're talking about."

Why, then, had the Hunter been summoned?

"What's supposed to happen after I get here—can you remember?"

The director shook his head. He almost looked relieved. It was as if he had the feeling that, if he became involved with this young man in any way, there'd be a terrible price to pay later.

D drifted toward the door. He didn't give another glance to the girl or the hospital director. He was about to leave. There was nothing here to hold a Vampire Hunter's interest.

Wanting to say something to him, the director realized he really had nothing to say. There were no words to address a shadow. When the door finally closed, the director wasn't completely sure that he'd actually met the young man.

On his way through the lobby to the exit, D passed a man. He was middle-aged and dressed in a cotton shirt and trousers and, while both garments were clean, they'd also been patched countless times. His rugged face had been carved by the brutal elements. Anyone could easily picture him out working the soil to earn his daily bread. With a weary expression, he quickly walked past D.

Slipping once more through the feverish gazes of the nurse and patients, D exited the lobby. Silently riding down the slope, he came to a little road. It wouldn't be much farther to the main road. But, just as he was going around a curve at the bottom of the hill, he found a dragon-drawn wagon coming from the opposite direction.

Not all of the supernatural creatures and demons the Nobility had unleashed were necessarily ferocious beasts. Though extremely rare, there were certain species, like sprites and smaller dragons, that humans could keep. Some of these creatures could howl for flames in freezing winter or summon the rains that were indispensable for raising produce, while others could replace machinery as a source of cheap labor. The beast before D now was a perfect example of the latter.

The dragon seemed to have sensed D even before it saw him. Its bronze flesh was covered with bumps that manifested its fear, and not even the whip of the farmer in the driver's seat could make it budge.

After lashing the beast a number of times, the farmer gave up, throwing down the whip and drawing the electronic spear from a holster beside his seat. As he hit the switch, it released a spring inside the handle. A three-foot-long spear suddenly telescoped out to twice that size. At the same time, the battery kicked in and the steel tip gave off a pale blue glow.

The weapon was far more powerful than its appearance suggested—even if it didn't break the skin, the mere touch of it would deliver a jolt of fifty thousand volts. According to the *Complete Frontier Encyclopedia*, it was effective against all but the top fifty of the two hundred most vicious creatures in the midsize class. While jabbing a beast of burden in the haunches with it might be a bit rough, the technique certainly wasn't unheard of. The dragon's hindquarters were swollen with dark red wounds where it'd been stabbed before. Electromagnetic waves tinged the sunlight blue. The farmer's eyes bulged from their sockets, but the dragon didn't budge.

No amount of training could break a dragon's wild urges. Cyborg horses were something the dragons loved to prey on, but, even with one nearby, there wasn't the slightest glimmer of savagery in the beast's eyes. It remained transfixed, and tinged with fear. It couldn't pull away . . . It stood still as a statue, almost like a beautiful woman enthralled by a demon.

As D passed, the farmer clucked his tongue in disgust and pulled back his spear. Since his cart was so large, there were fewer than three feet left to squeeze by on the side of the road. The point of his spear swung around. An instant later, it was shooting out at full speed toward D's back.

III

The blue magnetic glow never would've suspected that at the very last second a flash of silver would drop down from above to challenge it. D's pose didn't change in the least as his right hand drew his blade and sent the front half of the spear sailing through the air.

Still leaning forward from his thrust, the farmer barely managed to pull himself straight. The farmer, after only a moment's pause, made a ferocious leap from the driver's seat. In midair, he drew the broadsword he wore through the back of his belt. When he brought the blade down with a wide stroke, a bloody mist danced out in the sunlight.

Looking only for an instant at the farmer who'd fallen to the ground with a black arrowhead poking out of the base of his neck, D turned his eyes to what he'd already computed to be the other end of that trajectory. There was only an expanse of blue sky . . . But the steel arrow stuck through the farmer's neck had flown from somewhere up there.

The stink of blood mixed with the almost stifling aroma of greenery in the air, and, as D sat motionless on his steed, the sunlight poured down on him. There wasn't a second attack.

Finally, D dropped his gaze to the farmer lying on the ground, just to be sure of something. The bloodstained arrow was the same deadly implement the man had used to attack him in his dream. Perhaps the arrow had flown *from* the world of dreams.

Putting his longsword back in its sheath, in a low voice D asked, "You saw what happened, didn't you?"

Behind him, someone seemed to be surprised. Just around the base of the hill, a slim figure sat astride a motorbike of some kind, rooted to the spot. The reason her long hair swayed was because her whole body was trembling.

"Uh, yes," she said, nodding slowly. It was the same young woman who'd told him to go to the hospital.

"Tell the sheriff exactly what you saw," D said tersely, giving a kick to the belly of his horse.

"Wait—you can't go. You have to talk to the sheriff," the girl cried passionately. "If you don't, the law will be after you until the whole situation gets sorted out. You plan on running the rest of your life? Don't worry. I saw the whole thing. And don't you wanna get to the bottom of this mystery? Find out why everyone dreamed about you?"

The cyborg horse stopped in its tracks.

"To be completely honest," the girl continued, "that wasn't the first time I'd seen your face, either. I've met you plenty of times. In my dreams. So I knew about you a long time before everyone else did. I knew you'd come for sure. That's why I came after you."

Up in the saddle, D turned and looked back at her.

Though the girl had no idea she'd just done the impossible, her eyes were gleaming. "Great. I'm glad you changed your mind. It might be my second time seeing you, but, anyway, nice to meet you. I'm Nan Lander."

"Call me D."

"Kind of a strange name, but I like it. It's like the wind." Though she'd intended that as a compliment, D was as uncongenial as ever, and, with a troubled expression, Nan said, "I'll hurry off and fetch the sheriff." And with that, she steered her motorbike back around the way she'd come.

Due to urgent business, the sheriff wasn't in, but a young deputy quickly wrapped up the inquiry. D was instructed not to leave town for the time being. The deputy said the farmer who'd been killed was named Tokoff, and he had lived on the outskirts of the village. He was a violent man prone to drunken rages, and they'd planned on bringing him in sooner or later, which explained why the matter of his death could be settled so easily. Even more fortunate was the fact that he didn't have any family.

"But for all that, he wasn't the kind of man to go around indiscriminately throwing spears at folks, either. If we didn't have Nan's word for it, your story would be mighty hard to believe. We're gonna have to check into your background a wee bit." The trepidation in the deputy's voice was due, no doubt, to the fact he'd already heard D's name. But that was probably also the reason why he'd accepted the surreal tale of Tokoff being slain by an arrow fired from nowhere at all after attacking the Hunter.

Nan said she'd show D the way to the hotel. The two of them were crossing the creaky floor on the way to the door when D asked in a low voice, "Did you dream about me, too?"

A few seconds later, the deputy replied, "Yep." But his voice just rebounded off the closed door.

With Nan at the fore, the two of them started walking down the street, D leading his horse while she pushed her bike. The wind, which had grown fiercer, threw up gritty clouds that sealed off the world with white.

"You . . . you didn't ask him anything at all about Tokoff," Nan said as she gazed at D with a mournful look in her eye. "Didn't ask the name of the man you killed, or his line of work, or if he had a family. Don't you care? Does it just not matter now that he's dead? You don't even wonder why he attacked you, do you? I can't see how you can live that way."

Perhaps it was her earnestness rather than her censure that moved D's lips. "You should think about something else," he said.

"I suppose you're right," Nan replied, letting the subject go with unexpected ease.

On the Frontier, it was taboo to show too much interest in travelers, or any concern for them. Perhaps it was the enthusiasm all too common in girls her age that made her forget for a brief instant the rule that'd been borne not out of courtesy, but from the very real need to prevent crimes against those who would bare their souls to strangers.

D halted. They were in front of a bar. It was just a little before twelve o'clock Noon. Beyond the batwing doors, women who looked to be housewives could be seen clustered around the tables.

Under extreme circumstances or in impoverished Frontier villages that lacked other recreation facilities, this one institution— the bar—often played a part in essentially everything the villagers did. The bar served a number of purposes—a casino for the men, a coffee shop and chat room for housewives, and a reading room and a place to exchange information on fashion and discuss matters of the heart for young ladies. It wasn't even frowned on when the tiniest of tots tried their hand at gambling. For that reason, the bar was open all day long.

Nan watched with a hardened expression as D wrapped the reins around a fence in front of the building. "Aren't we going to your hotel to talk? I wouldn't mind. It's not like I wanna be a kid forever."

Giving her no reply, D stepped up onto the raised wooden sidewalk. He didn't even look at Nan.

The girl gnawed her lip. She wanted to look him square in the face so she could glare at him. All the anger she could muster was directed at his black-clad back, but the wind that came gusting by at that moment lifted the hem of his coat to deflect her rage. When she pushed her way through the doors a moment later, she found the figure in black was already seated at a table right by the counter.

From the far left corner of the bar, where all the housewives congregated, D was being bombarded with whispers and glances. Every gaze was strangely feverish, yet filled with fear at the same time. Everyone could tell. Everyone could see this young man belonged to another world.

Feeling a certain relief at D's choice of table, Nan took a seat directly across from him. Telling the sleepy-eyed bartender on the other side of the counter, "Paradigm cocktail, please," she looked at D.

"Shangri-La wine," was all D said, and the bartender gave a nod and turned around.

"You know, you're a strange one," Nan said, her tone oddly gloomy. "You can watch someone get killed without even raising an eyebrow, but you won't take a woman back to your room. On the other hand, you did get me a grown-up seat here. Are all Vampire Hunters like you?"

"My line of work was in your dream, too?"

Nan nodded. "Even though you didn't come out and say it, I just knew. And I knew you'd come here, too. Though I didn't know exactly *when* it would be."

"You know why you had that dream?"

Nan shook her head. "Can anyone tell you why they dream what they do?" Quickly donning an earnest expression that suited a young lady, Nan added, "But I understand. I saw that you were just walking on and on in this blue light. Where you came from, where you were going—no, scratch the first part. I only knew where you were going. To see Sybille. And there's your answer."

Was she trying to suggest the sleeping girl had summoned him? Why would Sybille do that? And why had only Nan seen D over and over again? The mystery remained.

"Thirty years ago, she was bitten by a Noble. The doctor said it was only natural you'd tell me to go to the hospital. Why are you so concerned about her?"

"Why did Sybille call you here, for that matter? How come I'm the only one who's dreamed about you more than once? I'm going to be honest with you—I'm so scared, I can't stand it." There was a hint of urgency in Nan's voice. "No matter how scary a dream may be, you can forget it after you open your eyes. Real life is a lot more painful. But this time, I'm just as scared after I wake up. No, I'm even more scared . . . " Her voice failed.

The millions of words embedded in the silence that followed were shattered with D's next remark. "This village is the only place where humans and Nobility lived and worked together on equal terms," he said. "I hear they aren't around any more, but I'd like to know what it used to be like."

For a second, Nan focused a look of horrible anger at the Hunter's gorgeous face, and then she shook her head. "You won't get that from me. If that's what interests you, old Mrs. Sheldon could tell you plenty."

"Where can I find her?"

"The western edge of the village. Just follow the orchards, and you'll find the place soon enough. Why? Is something going on?" Nan asked, leaning over the table.

"Hell, we'd like to know that, too!"

As the rough voice drifted across the bar, a number of figures spread out in the room, too. The batwing doors swung wildly, hinges creaking.

"Mr. Clements."

Nan's eyes reflected a man baring his teeth—a man who looked like a brick wall someone had dressed in a leather vest. It wasn't just the material forming the contours of the secondhand combat suit he wore that made him look more than six and a half feet tall—the massive frame of the man inside the combat suit was imposing in both size and shape.

A killing lust had taken over the bar. The housewives were a sickly hue as they got to their feet. In addition to the man called Clements, there were six others. All of them wore power-amplifying combat suits.

"Mr. Clements, we don't want any trouble here . . . " the bartender called out fretfully from behind the counter as he loaded glasses onto a tray.

"Go out back for a while, Jatko," the giant said in a weighty tone. There was a little gray mixed in his hair, but he looked like he could strangle a bear even without his combat suit. "Tally up yesterday's take or something. We'll pay you for anything that gets broken. Nan, you'd best run along, too. You start getting friendly with these drifter types, and you're not gonna be too popular around town."

"I can talk to whomever I please," Nan retorted, loudly enough for everyone to hear.

"Well, we'll discuss that matter later. Move it!" Clements tossed his jaw in Nan's direction, and a man to his left went into action. An arm empowered with hundreds of times its normal strength grabbed Nan by the shoulder.

Suddenly, her captor's face warped in pain. Oddly enough, neither the men there nor even Nan had noticed until now that D had stood up.

A black glove held the wrist of the man's combat suit. The man's body shook, but D didn't move in the slightest. It looked like his hand was just gently resting on the other man. But what was gentle for this young man was cause for others to shudder.

The Hunter moved his hand easily, and the arm of the combat suit went along with it as it limned a semicircle. "This young lady came in here with me," the Hunter said. "It would be best if she leaves with me, too." And then D calmly brought his hand down, and the sound of bones snapping echoed through the quiet bar.

Clements looked scornfully at his lackey, who'd fainted dead away from the pain. "Beat by a damn Hunter. That really makes me sick," he spat, gazing at D. "Stanley Clements is the name—I head up the local Vigilance Committee and breed guard beasts. I'm a big deal in these parts, if I do say so myself. You remember that when you tangle with me."

D was silent.

Perhaps mistaking silence for fright, Clements continued. "We hear tell you killed Tokoff. For a lousy drifter, you've got a lot of nerve laying a hand on a clean-living villager," Clements said, his voice brimming with confidence.

"That's not how it was, Mr. Clements. I saw the whole thing. And Bates agreed, too. He's not the one who shot that arrow, I tell you!"

Ignoring Nan's desperate explanation, Clements sneered, "I don't know what the hell that deputy told you, but you're gonna leave town quick. After we have a little fun with you, that is."

It seemed Nan had a good deal more courage than the average person. The girl reprovingly interjected the comment, "Orders from Mr. Bates are as good as orders from the sheriff. You know, you're all gonna catch hell when he gets back."

"Shut your hole, you little brat!" Clements barked as rage gave a vermilion tinge to his already demonic visage. "Go ahead and take 'im!"

With that command, three men in combat suits charged at D. They didn't give the slightest consideration to the fact that he had Nan with him.

No sooner had D pushed the girl away than he was swallowed by a wave of orange armor. Nan's eyes were open as wide as they could go. Look at that. Didn't all three Vigilance Committee members just sail through the air and slam against the floor with an enormous crash? Weren't they supposed to have the strength of five hundred men in that armor?

If by some chance there'd been a super-high-speed camera there to film this scene, it would've caught D as he slipped between the jumbled forms of the trio and twisted their wrists behind their backs with secret skill. The wrist and shoulder joints of every last man were shattered beyond repair. Of course, even a dhampir was no match for the strength of a combat suit. In addition to the ancient technique he used to turn his opponents' strength and speed against themselves, he must've called on all his inhuman strength. But executing those moves with absolute perfection was something this young man alone could've done.

"Well, ain't that something," Clements groaned, growing pale as he did so. But he hadn't yet lost the will to fight. He still had two lackeys left. Slowly, they inched forward.

It was then that a composed voice declared, "That'll be enough of that."

"Sheriff!" Nan shouted with delight. The men in orange stopped what they were doing and closed their eyes. The fight that'd burned in them like a madness left like a dream.

"Who started this, Nan?" asked the tall shadow standing in front of the doors.

"Mr. Clements."

"You've got it all wrong, Krutz," the giant growled, vehemently refuting the charge as he turned to the lawman. "You gonna believe this little bitch? I swear to hell, I've been true to my word to you."

"In that case, I want you to resign as head of the vigilance committee right this minute," the man in the topcoat said. The silver star on his chest reflected Clements' anger-twisted features.

"C'mon, Krutz, I was just—"

"Take your men and clear out of here. You should thank him for throwing your boys so neatly. Today you get off without paying any damages."

Hesitating a bit, the giant started to walk out with his head hung low. The other two men followed closely behind him, with their four injured cohorts leaning on their shoulders for support. They banged out through the doors without a parting remark.

"Welcome back, Sheriff," Nan said, joy and trust suffusing her countenance as she greeted him. "You take care of that case already?"

"No. Truth is, I was just on my way home now. Have a little work in the fields that needs doing, you know." The sheriff's stern visage smiled wryly, and then he nodded to D. "Just glad I was able to keep this acquaintance of yours out of trouble." To the Hunter, he added, "Though there could've been a hundred of them up against you and they still wouldn't have had a chance."

The first time D had seen this man, he probably hadn't realized the other man's position, as Krutz hadn't been wearing his badge then. His face—placid, yet imbued with strength and iron will—belonged to the man the Hunter had passed in the hall back at the hospital.

With a polite tip of the head to D, he said, "I heard about the situation from Bates. Though I need you to stick around for a while, I'd like you to keep out of trouble if you can. I'll put the word out, but every village has a couple of characters who like to beat up folks on the sly." And then, his magnificent facade broke a little as he added, "Of course, any cuss stupid enough to go after you won't live long enough to regret it."

Nan was watching D as if waiting for some favorable reply, but the Hunter was as emotionless as ever when he stated, "I have no business here in town. I'll thank you to be fast about confirming my identity."

"Already done," Sheriff Krutz said, as he watched D with a calm gaze. "You can't very well live on the Frontier without knowing the name of Vampire Hunter D. I've met folks you helped before. What do you suppose they had to say about you?"

The black shadow slipped between the sheriff and the girl without a sound. "I'll be in the hotel." That was all they heard him say through the batwing doors that swayed closed behind him.

"Wait," the sheriff said, his gnarled fingers catching hold of Nan's shoulder as she was about to go after the Hunter.

"But I have to talk to him. It's about my dreams."

"You think talking's gonna solve all this?"

Nan suddenly let her shoulders drop. Her obsessive gaze stayed trained on what lay beyond the door. The sunlight swayed languidly. It was afternoon light.

"You keep away from him, understand me?" Nan heard the sheriff say, though he sounded miles away. "That's one dangerous man. Getting close to him won't bring you nothing but misery . . . Particularly if you're a woman."

"You said you'd met people he'd helped, didn't you?" Nan said absentmindedly. "What did they have to say about him?"

The sheriff shook his head. It was ominously slow as it moved from side to side. "Not a thing. They'd all just keep quiet and stare out the door or down the road. That must've been the way he'd gone when he left. And it'll be the same when he leaves our village, too."

"When he leaves here . . . " Nan's eyes were dyed the same color as the sunlight.

The sheriff pondered the next thing she said for quite a while after that, but in the end he still didn't understand what she meant.

"Before he could leave, he had to come," Nan said. "Had to come here, to this village."

Continued in

VAMPIRE HUNTER D

VOLUME 5
THE STUFF OF DREAMS

Now available from Dark Horse Books
and Digital Manga Publishing

ABOUT THE AUTHOR

Hideyuki Kikuchi was born in Chiba, Japan in 1949. He attended the prestigious Aoyama University and wrote his first novel *Demon City Shinjuku* in 1982. Over the past two decades, Kikuchi has authored numerous horror novels, and is one of Japan's leading horror masters, writing novels in the tradition of occidental horror authors like Fritz Leiber, Robert Bloch, H. P. Lovecraft, and Stephen King. As of 2004, there were seventeen novels in his hugely popular ongoing Vampire Hunter D series. Many live action and anime movies of the 1980s and 1990s have been based on Kikuchi's novels.

ABOUT THE ILLUSTRATOR

Yoshitaka Amano was born in Shizuoka, Japan. He is well known as a manga and anime artist and is the famed designer for the Final Fantasy game series. Amano took part in designing characters for many of Tatsunoko Productions' greatest cartoons, including *Gatchaman* (released in the U.S. as *G-Force* and *Battle of the Planets*). Amano became a freelancer at the age of thirty and has collaborated with numerous writers, creating nearly twenty illustrated books that have sold millions of copies. Since the late 1990s Amano has worked with several American comics publishers, including DC Comics on the illustrated Sandman novel *Sandman: The Dream Hunters* with Neil Gaiman and *Elektra and Wolverine: The Redeemer* with best-selling author Greg Rucka.